W9-BIR-148

PRAISE FOR ERIC LAROCCA

"A startling affair...I'll be cleaning up particles of darkness in my office for weeks."

— JOSH MALERMAN (*BIRD BOX, INSPECTION*)

"When broken people do broken things - especially in the name of love - we all get broken, too. What starts as sweetly genteel swiftly descends into everything that's brutalizingly ugly about the abusive master/slave dynamic. A hauntingly elegant, masterfully written, and ultimately devastating indictment of cruel manipulation and even crueler submission. This is one deeply fucked-up heartbreaker. You have been warned."

— JOHN SKIPP (*THE LIGHT AT THE END*)

"Part Dennis Cooper's *The Sluts,* part David Cronenberg's *The Brood*...Eric LaRocca's *Things Have Gotten Worse Since We Last Spoke* is a masterpiece of epistolary body horror."

— MAX BOOTH III (*WE NEED TO DO SOMETHING*)

THINGS HAVE GOTTEN WORSE SINCE WE LAST SPOKE

Eric LaRocca

Copyright © 2021 by Eric LaRocca, Artists, Weirdpunk Books

First Edition

WP-0012

Print ISBN 978-1-951658-12-0

Cover art by Kim Jakobsson (www.kimjakobssonart.com)

Cover Design by Ira Rat (www.filthyloot.com)

Editing and internal layout/formatting by Sam Richard

Weirdpunk Books logo by Nate Sorenson

Weirdpunk Books

www.weirdpunkbooks.com

To Ali, my love.
Things have gotten better since we first met.
You make me feel like less of a monster.

CONTENTS

AUTHOR'S NOTE

As there has already been an overwhelming amount of conjecture and vitriol – especially in the dominion of online discussion – regarding the untimely demise of Agnes Petrella at the age of twenty-four, the author of this text has tenderly and judiciously compiled the following content with the hope of enlightening the public by publishing the contents of her correspondence with Zoe Cross in the several months prior to her death.

Because the litigation surrounding Zoe Cross's case remains open at the time of this publication, certain elements of their communication have been redacted or censored at the behest of the Henley's Edge Police Department. The author has noticeably marked these redacted elements with [omitted.] The absent contents remain in the archives of the Henley's Edge Police Department and are strictly forbidden from being removed from their records.

The author wishes to extend their heartfelt gratitude to the Henley's Edge Police Department, specifically Captain Gregory Deacon and Judge Louis Urchek for their amenableness and unwavering support throughout the course of composing this publication.

Also, the author of this publication requests that the reader be cognizant of the fact that the author is in no way affiliated with either Zoe Cross's legal counsel or Agnes Petrella's surviving family. The author remains a nonpartisan entity and instead patiently waits for the balances of justice to tip in favor of the truth.

PART ONE
A SLICED APPLE

POST WRITTEN BY AGNES PETRELLA ON ONLINE QUEER COMMUNITY BOARD

[The following post was recovered from QueerList.org – a website where members, usually openly identifying members of the LGBTQ+ community, can converse and solicit. The author wishes to express their heartfelt gratitude to the website's chief administrator, Sig Thornton, for recovering the post from his well-organized archives and for being so remarkably generous throughout the research process.]

ANTIQUE APPLE PEELER WITH VIBRANT HISTORY FOR SALE

<u>Date:</u> Friday, May 26, 2000 at 3:47 pm EST
<u>User:</u> agnes_in_wonderland_76
<u>Asking Price:</u> $250 [will settle for $220]

I was going to begin this with some absurd comment about the irony of posting about an apple peeler in a queer discussion forum when most of us are probably triggered by the mere mention of the word "fruit."

I decided to begin with a story instead.

Every family has a myth for the young to inherit – an undocumented fable passed between mouths, a grave illness to be contracted – as if the very words were a blight to infect the youth with and let them know they're now welcome to the fold.

After all, what exactly is a family, if not a brotherhood and sisterhood afflicted with the same terminal disease?

When I was very young, my grandmother told me a story about how her mother – an immigrant from Naples – had desperately longed for a proper apple peeler in order to make a traditional apple pie.

The man she had married, though generous enough to gift her five children to carry in her belly over the course of six years, was resolute in his decision – he would not give her the money for the apple peeler no matter how much she begged.

So, my great-grandmother devised a plan to make her husband understand just how urgent she needed a peeler. Not only would her plan showcase her need, but it would stress a measure of safety as well.

The following day, my great-grandmother packed her husband's lunch pail and kissed him "goodbye" as he set off for work. She waited, spent the morning tailoring a suit for one of her neighbors. Finally, the news she had been waiting for arrived. One of the Carpino boys that lived next door showed up on her doorstep and explained how her husband had been taken to the local doctor.

"What for?" she had asked, her hands hiding the smile beginning to thaw across her face.

"Something he ate," the Carpino boy told her. "He bit into an apple with a sewing needle stuck inside."

A week later and my great-grandmother was at the local department store picking out an apple peeler, chaperoned by her dear husband with his jaw bandaged shut.

As you can already tell by the pictures attached to this thread [images omitted], this antique apple peeler has endured for over a century and provided sustenance for four generations of family members.

I've gone through various documents my grandmother had left me and consequently discovered a letter my great-grandmother had sent to her sister (who was living in Turin, Italy at the time) and she details going to the department store with her husband to pick out an apple peeler. The letter is dated August the 5th, 1897. So, that means, in no uncertain times, the apple peeler was manufactured in 1897. Possibly even earlier – 1896. I can happily scan a copy of the letter and include it with the item for the sake of verifying the appliance's authenticity. I'm also more than happy to send along a copy of the letter for a historian to verify prior to purchase.

You might be interested to know not only was the apple peeler's purchase of the sordid variety, but the appliance furnished the hands of one of the state of Connecticut's beloved composers – Charles Ives. My grandmother, frequently guilty of repeating the same story at a family gathering on separate occasions, would often regale those who were patient enough to listen more than once with the story of how the apple peeler was once used by Charles Ives, a family friend, at a picnic in 1948 – the very year after he had won the Pulitzer Prize.

Unfortunately, there's no way to authenticate this claim that the apple peeler was once used by Mr. Ives. On two separate occasions, I have scoured my parents' basement in search of photographs documenting the picnic and found no evidence of Mr. Ives at a family picnic in the late 1940's. In an effort to be as transparent with you as possible, my grandmother was prone to manufacturing stories that she imagined might titillate her guests. She once told a family friend that Marcello Mastroianni (you might remember him from *La Dolce Vita*) was a distant family relation on her mother's side. Her stories became more fanciful and varied in her old age; however, she clung to the story of Charles Ives until the night the hospice nurses arrived.

Make of that what you will.

If you're in the market for a conversation starter, then look no further. I can't tell you the amount of times house guests have marveled at this particular antique appliance pinned to my kitchen wall. On more than three separate occasions I've had offers from guests to purchase the peeler; however, at the time, I couldn't bear to part with it.

If you're a serious collector with a fervent taste for traditional Americana – no pun intended – then this is the appliance for you. Be mindful that this appliance is still in proper working order. Though, a skilled owner will be aware not to overuse the tool as it requires the tenderness only a true collector possesses. It's my sincere hope that this apple peeler go to a considerate and thoughtful owner, eager to add a touch of history to their beautiful home, or perhaps to add another excellent addition to their growing collection.

Feel free to email me: agnes_in_wonderland_76@[omitted].com with any further questions. I'm delighted to help in any way I can. Please do not contact me with unsolicited services or offers.

Please be advised, once purchased I will not accept returns or issue refunds.

EMAIL FROM ZOE CROSS

[The following pages contain the first correspondence between Zoe Cross and Agnes Petrella. As mentioned in the Author's Note, certain sections of the email correspondence have been truncated or omitted entirely as Ms. Cross's case is still pending an investigation.]

Date: 05/28/2000
Time: 12:09 p.m.
From: Zoe Cross <crushedmarigolds@[omitted].com>
To: Agnes Petrella
<agnes_in_wonderland_76@[omitted].com>
Subject: Re: Antique Apple Peeler with Vibrant History for Sale

Dear Agnes,

While I don't claim to possess the refinement of a serious antique collector, I'm filled with the same urgency of your great-grandmother to acquire something very near and dear to my heart. My grandfather is turning ninety-two during the month of July. He's especially fond of the work of composer Charles Ives and, quite frankly, I had to do a double take when I first read your original post because it seemed too serendipitous – too good to be true.

Although it's unfortunate you can't prove the appliance was once in the possession of Mr. Ives at a family picnic, I think my grandfather would be tickled to know of the story and would appreciate the appliance with or without the proper proof.

My grandfather, a World War Two veteran, doesn't talk much about his involvement with the war; however, he has mentioned time and time again how the Lieutenants in the garrisons would often play Ives on the radio. In fact, one of my earliest memories of my grandfather – other than his distinct smell of lavender – involves me sitting on his lap on the front porch of his house in Revere, MA as a Charles Ives record played.

I understand in your original post you had stressed the importance of the appliance going to the home of a serious collector. Unfortunately, I cannot pretend to claim my grandfather is a dedicated collector. In fact, with his health failing, it's more than likely that the appliance will be in his possession for a few years – maybe even months if his current doctor's prognosis proves to be true – before it's inherited by one of the younger members of our family. Possibly myself.

That's not to say that my grandfather does not covet his belongings with the tenderness and care of an antiquarian specialist. My grandfather recently purchased a Harpers Ferry Model 1855 musket at a public auction in Danvers, MA. He's since cared for the rifle as if it were his only child. I visit him occasionally on the weekends when I can comfortably make the trek from Cambridge to Springfield and typically find him hunched over his prized possession, hands furiously polishing the barrel with a cloth.

If you were to sell the antique apple peeler to me – and I wholeheartedly understand if you carry some reservations given the questionable longevity of my grandfather's health – I can assure you the appliance will be well looked after. If not by my grandfather, then by me personally. As I had explained, I don't pretend to be an antique specialist; however, I can assure you I make good word of my promises. Of course, you're more than likely hesitant to accept such a statement from a complete stranger on the internet. Regardless, the apple peeler will be finding a good home.

If you haven't tossed my email in the trash by now, perhaps we could discuss the matter of the price. According to your post, you're seeking $250, but will settle for $220. I think that's more than agreeable given the rich history surrounding the appliance. After all, it's still in working order!

Would you be receptive to offering express shipping at no additional cost if I offered to pay the desired $250? It would certainly help my pocketbook.

Of course, I completely understand if that's not possible. We can negotiate at a later date.

Regardless, please let me know if you are open to the idea of selling the apple peeler to me. I would be more than delighted to take it off your hands and offer it the best home I can afford.

I look forward to hearing from you.

Best regards,
Zoe

EMAIL FROM AGNES PETRELLA

Date: 05/29/2000
Time: 10:43 a.m.
From: Agnes Petrella <agnes_in_wonderland_76@[omit-ted].com>
To: Zoe Cross <crushedmarigolds@[omitted].com>
Subject: Re: Antique Apple Peeler with Vibrant History for Sale

Dear Zoe,

Thank you so much for reaching out and for writing such a thoughtful email. Most of the responses I've been receiving on the post have unfortunately been solicitations for activities I can't even imagine having the determination to write down, let alone engage in. Your email was a much welcome respite from a seemingly never-ending onslaught of rudeness.

So, thank you for that.

Based on the thoughtfulness of your email and the dedication you put into crafting your inquiry, I am most certainly open to the idea of selling you the apple peeler. Although my original post may have stressed the importance of the new owner possessing a certain skillset in order to appropriately take care of the appliance, much of that was said in order to suitably vet the contacts who might attempt to query me.

As you can probably tell from my original post, this apple peeler means a great deal to me. It's been in my family for many generations and was passed down to me by my mother. If possible, I would like for it to become a treasured item belonging to another family – a precious relic to become a birthright for a new generation. I don't anticipate having children of my own, so I would hope that the apple peeler might go to a home burgeoning with little ones. Of course, I understand this may not be possible. Despite my wishes, I think your grandfather would take excellent care of the apple peeler.

If you'd like, I would be happy to include a small note in the parcel detailing my grandmother's account of Charles Ives at the family picnic. I only wish I could prove the report. But, as you said, your grandfather will appreciate the appliance with or without the proof.

To answer your question regarding express shipping at no additional cost, I would be more than happy to offer to send the parcel at an expedited rate at no additional cost if you purchase the item at the requested $250. I think that would be more than agreeable. Plus, I hardly expected I would find somebody as caring and as devoted to their family as you.

It's my pleasure to sell the apple peeler to you, especially knowing how fond your grandfather is of Charles Ives. Isn't that perfect?

I must admit, I'm slightly hesitant to sell the appliance in general considering how precious it has been to me over the years. It's really the only thing my mother has ever given me. Not to mention, it's something my grandmother touted as a magical instrument when I was little. I used to foolishly think it could grant wishes.

I guess we all have things from our childhood we eventually have to let go of.

Please send me your mailing address after you've sent the payment and we'll go from there.

Again, thank you so much for your thoughtfulness. It means so much to me.

Best regards,

Agnes

EMAIL FROM ZOE CROSS

Date: 05/29/2000
Time: 3:13 p.m.
From: Zoe Cross <crushedmarigolds@[omitted].com>
To: Agnes Petrella
<agnes_in_wonderland_76@[omitted].com>
Subject: Re: Antique Apple Peeler with Vibrant History for Sale

Dear Agnes,

I am overjoyed to know you're willing to sell me the apple peeler, especially with the requested expedited shipping at no additional cost. I was hesitant – perhaps nervous as well – to send you my initial email as I worried I wouldn't be an adequate candidate for your item, but I'm so delighted to hear you're receptive to my offer.

I plan to send the money to your bank tomorrow afternoon when the funds appear in my account after I make the necessary transfer.

I hope you'll excuse my momentary forwardness with you, but I'm curious to know why you're selling the apple peeler in the first place if it holds such profound emotional value to you. I have to admit – I'm hesitant to make the purchase of the item if you're on the fence about selling.

I would hate to think I'm robbing you of some dearly cherished, irreplaceable artifact.

Best,

Zoe

EMAIL FROM AGNES PETRELLA

Date: 05/30/2000
Time: 8:32 a.m.
From: Agnes Petrella <agnes_in_wonderland_76@[omitted].com>
To: Zoe Cross <crushedmarigolds@[omitted].com>
Subject: Re: Antique Apple Peeler with Vibrant History for Sale

Zoe,

I sincerely appreciate your thoughtfulness during this difficult time. I don't consider your email to be too forward at all, considering how vulnerable I made myself during my original online post. I wholeheartedly understand your concern to purchase now, especially after I've expressed how precious the appliance was – and still is – to me and my family.

The truth is this apple peeler is one of the few things I

ERIC LAROCCA

have left of my grandmother. She passed away when I was
a teenager and had always joked that this apple peeler was
to serve as my dowry. When I moved out on my own –
into my first apartment – it was one of the few things my
mother could afford to give me as a housewarming
present. Something I had treasured for so many years – a
reminder of the generous and beautiful spirit my grandmother once was.

That night, my mother and I peeled apples to make a
pie. We ate cookies with vanilla frosting until two in the
morning.

The fact is that was the last night my mother and I
laughed together. Or even hugged, for that matter.

You see, when I left home for the first time, I made a
promise to myself that I would live as authentically as I
possibly could. No matter the consequences.

So, I did.

I picked up the phone and I called my mom and I said,
"Mom, there's something I need to tell you and Dad."

She exhaled; the dim rumbling of her breath clogging
in the pit of her throat sounded like a thunderstorm
breaking apart as it passed through a stretch of mountains.

I waited until I could hear my father milling about in
the background, close enough to hear what I had to say.

Finally, I said it: "Mom, Dad. I'm gay."

There was a long, painful pause, and I recall I could
feel my heartbeat hammering in the space between my ears
– the blood rushing to my face and pooling there as
violently as whitewater rapids.

Finally, my mother spoke. "My child isn't gay."

And she hung up.

That was the very last thing she said to me. I haven't talked to her in two years.

The apple peeler was one of the last things she had given me before we stopped talking – something I thought I would keep as a memory of my family until I had a family of my own one day. But that doesn't seem that likely anymore.

You had asked me why exactly I was selling the apple peeler if it held such a profound sentimental value. The truth is I would keep it if I could. I don't want to bore you with the details or throw myself a little pity party, but I've been struggling to make my rent payment for the last several months because of a pay cut I had to take at my job. The extra $250 would really help me out this coming month and keep me afloat so I can bide my time before I can figure out what I'm going to do next.

I had never planned to reveal exactly why I was planning to sell the apple peeler to whoever I arranged to purchase the item. But you seem so genuine and so thoughtful. I know you won't judge me or think ill of me for discarding such a precious remnant of my family's history.

I assure you I would never accept your money if I knew in my heart I could not bear to part with it. More importantly, I promise to not pester you after the purchase and make certain the apple peeler is being well cared for. Once we make the transaction, that's it. I trust that the apple peeler will be going to a good home with you and your grandfather. I have no reservations to sell. If it seems like I am somewhat hesitant, it's merely because it feels like I'm holding a funeral for my former self – the person I was before I lived with integrity and honesty. It's the funeral for a person I wouldn't want you to know.

After all, I much prefer who I am now.

Well, sometimes I do.

Although I must confess – I sometimes wonder how I'll properly peel apples without it. I suppose the Greek philosopher, Epicurus, was right – "A free life cannot acquire many possessions, because this is not easy to do without servility to mobs or monarchs."

Best,

Agnes

EMAIL FROM ZOE CROSS

Date: 05/31/2000
Time: 9:24 a.m.
From: Zoe Cross <crushedmarigolds@[omitted].com>
To: Agnes Petrella
<agnes_in_wonderland_76@[omitted].com>
Subject: Re: Antique Apple Peeler with Vibrant History for Sale

Agnes,

Once again, I hope you'll excuse my forwardness when I ask for your bank account routing information so that I can wire your monthly rent payment to you. I know we don't even really know one another, but I recognize when I've been blessed with certain things others have not.

I would be remiss if I did not take this opportunity to help you in the way that you so clearly need it. I'm lucky enough to never have to worry about rent payment or whether or not I'll survive another bill cycle, and I would be honored to help you do the same.

I know you'll probably be hesitant – you'll probably insist that you don't need the assistance. I would ask you to reconsider your stubbornness and accept help when it's offered so freely and so selflessly.

I would also like to take this opportunity to give you my Instant Messenger contact information in case you ever need to talk. You can find me at <crushedmarigolds>. I'm usually online later at night as I typically work remotely during the day.

Please never hesitate to reach out or ask for help if you need it. As I said before, I know we're complete strangers to one another, but I truly believe I'm within my right to help another human being when I can see clearly that they're struggling.

Talk soon,

Zoe

EMAIL FROM AGNES PETRELLA

Date: 05/31/2000
Time: 11:12 a.m.
From: Agnes Petrella <agnes_in_wonderland_76@[omitted].com>
To: Zoe Cross <crushedmarigolds@[omitted].com>
Subject: Re: Antique Apple Peeler with Vibrant History for Sale

Zoe,

I'm so shocked by your generosity. I really don't quite know what to say. I've, of course, heard of things like this happening to people. But never in my wildest dreams did I ever think it would happen to me.

Normally I would pretend to resist slightly or make up some nonsensical excuse as to why I couldn't possibly accept your offer.

I'm afraid I'm at such a loss for words I can barely think of anything to say other than "yes."

I'm a bit hesitant to give out my private information over email, but I know full well you won't be able to rob me. There's hardly anything left in my account. I spent all I had left yesterday on groceries for the rest of the week.

I didn't know how I was going to pay the month of June's rent to be quite frank. It was the first time in my life I had thought of doing horrible things to actually get a paycheck.

My bank routing information is as follows:

[omitted]

Once again, I don't quite know what to say.

I've been called many things over the years, but "speechless" has seldom been one of them. I don't quite know what I could ever do to repay you for your kindness, but I'll think of something. Maybe we'll be able to meet up one day so I can properly thank you in person.

Again, thank you for your kindness. It means so much to me.

Your friend,

Agnes

EMAIL FROM AGNES PETRELLA

Date: 06/01/2000
Time: 10:46 a.m.
From: Agnes Petrella <agnes_in_wonderland_76@[omitted].com>
To: Zoe Cross <crushedmarigolds@[omitted].com>
Subject: THANK YOU!

THANK YOU FROM THE BOTTOM OF MY HEART!

I just called my bank and they notified me that the total sum of one thousand dollars had been wired to my account last night by a Ms. Zoe Cross.

I don't quite know what to say.

I never thought anything like this would ever happen in my life.

I owe you so much. I can't believe this is real.

Thank you. A million times.

Your friend,

Agnes xoxo

EMAIL FROM AGNES PETRELLA

Date: 06/01/2000
Time: 11:07 a.m.
From: Agnes Petrella <agnes_in_wonderland_76@[omitted].com>
To: Zoe Cross <crushedmarigolds@[omitted].com>
Subject: Re: THANK YOU!

OK. I've since calmed down since I sent my last email. Hopefully this one will be more coherent.

I really do owe you so much for your kindness, your generosity, etc.

I truly never thought something like this would ever happen to me. I don't have to go to bed tonight dreading tomorrow – waking up in a cold sweat and wondering if my check will bounce.

You really have changed my life.

I don't know what I could possibly ever do to repay you, but just know that you have changed the life of someone who was seriously contemplating ending it all if things kept going the way they were going.

It's not as if I had a plan or anything. I didn't go out and buy a rope or rat poison to stir in my morning coffee. But I was sincerely considering doing something to change my life in an irreversible way. You plucked me right from the edge before I was about to jump. I hope you know that.

I really can't thank you enough for what you've given me.

You've changed my life, guardian angel.

Your friend,

Agnes xoxo

EMAIL FROM ZOE CROSS

Date: 06/01/2000
Time: 2:39 p.m.
From: Zoe Cross <crushedmarigolds@[omitted].com>
To: Agnes Petrella
<agnes_in_wonderland_76@[omitted].com>

Subject: Re: THANK YOU!

Agnes,

Of course. It was my sincere pleasure.

I would be more than happy to lend a helping hand anytime you find yourself in a bind. This is not merely a one-time offer.

When you're gay, you have the privilege of choosing your family.

I learned quickly that blood is not always thicker than water. Sometimes the people that care for us the most are the people we least expect.

I, like you, have a responsibility to my fellow queer brothers and sisters to aid them with my blessings.

If you'd like to talk, I'll be on Instant Messenger tonight. We can talk more there.

Your friend,

Zoe

INSTANT MESSAGING CONVERSATION BETWEEN AGNES AND ZOE

[The following text is a transcript of a conversation between Agnes Petrella and Zoe Cross over Instant Messenger. Certain sections of the text have been censored or redacted at the request of the Henley's Edge Police Department. These censored areas have been marked with [omitted].*]*

06/01/2000

[<crushedmarigolds> has entered the chat]
[<agnes_in_wonderland_76> has entered the chat]

10:09:04 <crushedmarigolds> Hey

10:09:13 <agnes_in_wonderland_76> Hey

10:09: 19 <agnes_in_wonderland_76> I came earlier, but you weren't on yet

10:09: 29 <crushedmarigolds> Yeah, sorry. I was out for a bit. Couldn't get to the computer. Here now.

10:09: 40 <agnes_in_wonderland_76> I'm glad

10:10:01 <crushedmarigolds> Did you send the rent check to your landlord?

10:10:13 <agnes_in_wonderland_76> Took it to the post office this afternoon

10:10: 23 <crushedmarigolds> Good. I'm glad

10:10: 34 <agnes_in_wonderland_76> I really can't thank you enough

10:10:45 <crushedmarigolds> You think he'll be surprised?

10:10:57 <agnes_in_wonderland_76> I'm sure he was busy writing my eviction notice

10:11:22 <crushedmarigolds> You must be delighted to prove him wrong

10:11:48 <agnes_in_wonderland_76> I can't stop smiling. One of the women I worked with said she had never seen me happier.

10:11:56 <crushedmarigolds> I'm glad you're so happy

10:12:09 <agnes_in_wonderland_76> All thanks to you

10:12:31 <crushedmarigolds> Happy I could help in any way I could

10:12:48 <agnes_in_wonderland_76> I know I already said this, but you really did change my life.

10:12:58 <crushedmarigolds> I know

10:13:04 <agnes_in_wonderland_76> You really didn't have to do that

10:13:10 <crushedmarigolds> I wanted to

10:13:22 <crushedmarigolds> [omitted]

10:13:30 <agnes_in_wonderland_76> What are you doing right now?

10:13:42 <crushedmarigolds> Eating dinner, playing solitaire on the computer

10:13:51 <agnes_in_wonderland_76> Eating dinner this late?

10:14:02 <crushedmarigolds> Couldn't help it. I was busy all day

10:14:17 <crushedmarigolds> What are you doing?

10:14:29 <agnes_in_wonderland_76> Drinking a cup of tea, going to bed soon

10:14:42 <crushedmarigolds> Same. I can't stay on long. I have to get up early tomorrow

10:14:58 <agnes_in_wonderland_76> I wish you didn't have to

10:15:09 <crushedmarigolds> Me too. It's for work. Have to commute into the office

10:15:27 <agnes_in_wonderland_76> Will you be on tomorrow night?

10:15: 36 <crushedmarigolds> Definitely

10:15:49 <agnes_in_wonderland_76> Good

10:16:01 <crushedmarigolds> Will you make me a promise?

10:16:11 <agnes_in_wonderland_76> Anything

10:16:28 <crushedmarigolds> Don't sell the apple peeler. Keep it for your grandmother

10:16:39 <agnes_in_wonderland_76> OK. I will

10:16:52 <crushedmarigolds> We'll talk tomorrow?
10:17:01 <agnes_in_wonderland_76> Yeah, we'll talk tomorrow
10:17:08 <crushedmarigolds> Talk to you then
10:17:14 <agnes_in_wonderland_76> Talk to you

[<crushedmarigolds> has left the chat]
[<agnes_in_wonderland_76> has left the chat]

PART TWO

WHAT HAVE YOU DONE TODAY TO DESERVE YOUR EYES?

EMAIL FROM AGNES PETRELLA

Date: 06/03/2000
Time: 8:08 a.m.
From: Agnes Petrella <agnes_in_wonderland_76@[omitted].com>
To: Zoe Cross <crushedmarigolds@[omitted].com>
Subject: Thinking of you

I know you're probably busy at work, but I wanted to send you a quick note and let you know that you've been on my mind all morning.

Is that weird?

I hope it's not weird.

I once read somewhere that if your mind continuously returns to the same person over and over again, it means that they're thinking of you as well.

I hope that's true.

I'd be absolutely devastated to know it was a lie conjured by somebody who simply had too much time on their hands.

Of course, I'm certain you're busy. You probably don't have the luxury of endless free time to think. It's not that I have the luxury of endless time on my hands either. But I can't seem to compel my brain to think of anything other than you and your kindness.

Another user on that QueerList website reached out to me this morning and inquired if the apple peeler was for sale. You can imagine my surprise when I received the email. I thought I had taken the post down. I suppose in my excitement yesterday, the thought completely slipped my mind.

You'll be happy to know I've since taken down the listing from the website. The apple peeler is safe in its decorative place, pinned to my kitchen wall. In fact, I'm staring at it right now as I type this email.

I hope we have the chance to talk again later tonight. I like talking to you.

I feel more like myself when I talk to you. I don't quite know what it is.

Until then,

Agnes

EMAIL FROM ZOE CROSS

Date: 06/03/2000
Time: 1:07 p.m.
From: Zoe Cross <crushedmarigolds@[omitted].com>

<u>To:</u> Agnes Petrella
<agnes_in_wonderland_76@[omitted].com>
<u>Subject:</u> Re: Thinking of you

Agnes,

This will have to be a quick response as I'm currently swamped with work. But I wanted to take a moment and thank you for your email.

I'm delighted to hear you've removed your posting from the website and that the apple peeler is safe under your care. Well done. I wouldn't dream of having it any other way.

Unfortunately, I have plans for later this evening, so I won't be online much. I can certainly try to drop by around 11 o'clock or so if you'll still be awake.

I hope you will.

I look forward to it.

Zoe

INSTANT MESSAGING CONVERSATION BETWEEN AGNES AND ZOE

06/03/2000

[<crushedmarigolds> has entered the chat]
[<agnes_in_wonderland_76> has entered the chat]

11:04:05 <crushedmarigolds> Hey. You're still up
11:04:09 <crushedmarigolds> I'm glad
11:04:19 <agnes_in_wonderland_76> Can't stay long
11:04:28 <crushedmarigolds> I get it. It's late

11:04:39 <agnes_in_wonderland_76> Did you have fun?

11:04:44 <crushedmarigolds> Fun?

11:04:57 <agnes_in_wonderland_76> Wherever you were

11:05:09 <crushedmarigolds> I guess

11:05:18 <agnes_in_wonderland_76> Were you with someone else?

11:05:26 <crushedmarigolds> Someone else?

11:05:35 <agnes_in_wonderland_76> I know it's none of my business

11:05:47 <agnes_in_wonderland_76> Are you seeing someone?

11:05:52 <crushedmarigolds> I was.

11:05:58 <crushedmarigolds> Not anymore

11:06:08 <agnes_in_wonderland_76> Because something happened

11:06:12 <crushedmarigolds> Yes

11:06:19 <crushedmarigolds> Well, no

11:06:29 <agnes_in_wonderland_76> You can tell me

11:06:36 <crushedmarigolds> Because we were living past the expiration date

11:06:46 <agnes_in_wonderland_76> Were you with them tonight?

11:06:51 <crushedmarigolds> We ended it tonight

11:07:00 <agnes_in_wonderland_76> So… you were with her

11:07:06 <crushedmarigolds> Yeah

11:07:14 <crushedmarigolds> I didn't want to tell you

11:07:20 <agnes_in_wonderland_76> Why?

11:07:27 <crushedmarigolds> Thought it might spoil what we have

11:07:39 <agnes_in_wonderland_76> Is she there right now?

11:07:46 <crushedmarigolds> No. She left.

11:07:54 <crushedmarigolds> Gave me back her set of keys, too

11:08:01 <agnes_in_wonderland_76> Are you happy?

11:08:09 <crushedmarigolds> I will be someday

11:08:16 <agnes_in_wonderland_76> What are you doing right now?

11:08:25 <crushedmarigolds> Watching TV, eating some cereal

11:08:36 <agnes_in_wonderland_76> What are you watching?

11:08:42 <crushedmarigolds> Some travel program about Thailand

11:08:51 <crushedmarigolds> Did you know there's a place you can go to experience your own burial?

11:08:59 <crushedmarigolds> It's like a ritualized form of "pretend death."

11:09:09 <crushedmarigolds> You write your own eulogy, you're attended by a crowd of mourners

11:09:18 <crushedmarigolds> Then, you're interred in the earth for thirty minutes before you're exhumed

11:09:26 <agnes_in_wonderland_76> That's crazy

11:09:33 <crushedmarigolds> They give you an oxygen tank just in case, but I can't imagine doing it

11:09:39 <agnes_in_wonderland_76> Me neither

11:09:45 <crushedmarigolds> My father used to have a saying when I was really little...

11:09:52 <crushedmarigolds> At the end of each day, he used to ask me, "what have you done today to deserve your eyes?"

11:10:01 <crushedmarigolds> It took me years to understand what he actually meant

11:10:08 <crushedmarigolds> Our eyesight – among other things – is a gift that we take for granted

11:10:14 <crushedmarigolds> Right?

11:10:19 <agnes_in_wonderland_76> I suppose I haven't given it much thought

11:10:22 <crushedmarigolds> Exactly

11:10:29 <crushedmarigolds> It's not something we always think about until we lose it

11:10:38 <crushedmarigolds> We don't covet our hands until we lose a finger

11:10:43 <crushedmarigolds> We don't praise our hearing until we lose an ear

11:10:52 <crushedmarigolds> What have you done today to deserve your eyes?

11:11:04 <agnes_in_wonderland_76> You're asking me?

11:11:10 <crushedmarigolds> You can't answer, can you?

11:11:19 <agnes_in_wonderland_76> I guess I've never really thought about it

11:11:28 <crushedmarigolds> I'm going to hold you accountable from now on

11:11:37 <agnes_in_wonderland_76> Are you?

11:11:43 <crushedmarigolds> I'm going to check in each day and make certain you've done at least one thing to "deserve your eyes"

11:11:51 <crushedmarigolds> I'm not kidding

11:11:59 <agnes_in_wonderland_76> I believe you

11:12:07 <crushedmarigolds> I'm going to ask you start tomorrow

11:12:13 <agnes_in_wonderland_76> And how should I do that?

11:12:20 <crushedmarigolds> Where do you work?

11:12:29 <agnes_in_wonderland_76> [omitted]

11:12:36 <crushedmarigolds> It's an office building?

11:12:41 <agnes_in_wonderland_76> Yes. I'm one of the receptionists

11:12:50 <crushedmarigolds> You're going to make a statement

11:12:58 <agnes_in_wonderland_76> What kind of statement?

11:13:04 <crushedmarigolds> You're going to go out this weekend and buy a brand-new red dress

11:13:15 <crushedmarigolds> You're going to clip the tags so that you can't return it and you're going to wear it to work

11:13:21 <agnes_in_wonderland_76> A red dress at work? I'll be drawn and quartered

11:13:30 <crushedmarigolds> That's not all. You're going to buy a tube of blood red lipstick and wear it with your new dress

11:13:39 <agnes_in_wonderland_76> You must be out of your mind

11:13:47 <crushedmarigolds> I want you to take a picture of yourself in the employee bathroom and send it to me as proof

11:13:54 <agnes_in_wonderland_76> You've got to be joking

11:14:03 <crushedmarigolds> I'll be expecting the proof from you

11:14:12 <crushedmarigolds> I'll be expecting proof that you deserve your eyes

11:14:19 <crushedmarigolds> Do we have a deal?

11:14:29 <agnes_in_wonderland_76> I guess so

11:14:38 <crushedmarigolds> Perfect

11:14:45 <agnes_in_wonderland_76> I can't believe I'm

doing this
11:14:57 <crushedmarigolds> Pick the brightest, bloodiest red you can find
11:15:06 <crushedmarigolds> I'll talk to you tomorrow?
11:15:10 <agnes_in_wonderland_76> Yes. Talk to you tomorrow

[<crushedmarigolds> has left the chat]
[<agnes_in_wonderland_76> has left the chat]

EMAIL FROM AGNES PETRELLA

Date: 06/05/2000
Time: 7:12 p.m.
From: Agnes Petrella <agnes_in_wonderland_76@[omitted].com>
To: Zoe Cross <crushedmarigolds@[omitted].com>
Subject: The Red Dress

[Picture attached] [Omitted]

You'll be delighted to know that today I did the unthinkable.

I went to the department store during my lunch break and asked one of the sales associates where I could find the brightest, most garish red dress they had in stock. I was whisked away to the rear of the store by a short old woman who smelled of jasmine and pipe tobacco.

And there it was.

As decadently red as a severed artery in full bloom.

The old woman escorted me to the fitting room, and I

slipped the dress on as if it were a second layer of skin. I couldn't imagine taking it off. It felt so irresistibly perfect, as if it were the tightening embrace of a long lost loved one – someone I had met in a former life and was reunited with after centuries spent pining for their homecoming.

"Would you like to wear it out of the store?" the saleswoman asked me.

I caught my reflection in the paneled mirror at the end of the dressing room's corridor, and I do a double take because the girl I see standing there cannot possibly be me. She's smiling. She doesn't hide her lips behind trembling fingers as if her mouth were an untreated wound.

So, I passed my credit card to the saleswoman and she handed me a paper bag containing a neatly folded pile of my old clothes – the snakeskin I had molted and shed so effortlessly. And to think I could have done it this whole time. I cursed myself for being so contended, being so comfortable to remain as I once was – an insect burdened with a shell far too big for the smallness of their size.

But, before I left the store, I circled the makeup counter and peered through the collection of lipstick arranged in the case as if they were fine Parisian delicacies. I finally found the color I was looking for – "Red Velvet." I asked the saleswoman for the last tube of lipstick and she passed the small capsule to me. Angling the mirror on the counter toward me, I twisted the lipstick until it sprouted open and then smeared it across my lips until they were the dark color of a beetroot.

I returned to work and that's when I noticed that when you change, the people around you start to change as well. The arched eyebrows. The voices thinning to mere whispers. The spines straightening, faces blanching, as if I were brandishing a small weapon when I passed them. I suppose I was – the redness sprawling from every inch of my body as if I were blanketed with a rare tropical flower, a carnivorous plant with a decidedly avid appetite.

It wasn't long before one of the other secretaries – a woman I absolutely loathe with a short blonde pixie haircut – approached me at my desk and explained how my superior wanted to see me in her office at once.

So, I crept into her office and found her sitting there at her desk, sipping a cup of tea and waiting for me.

"Sit down, Agnes," she said, resting her cup of tea on a small saucer beside her pile of papers.

God, this can't be good, I thought to myself. Although I had expected attention for my new wardrobe choices, I hardly expected it would land me in my boss's office.

"We've had some – complaints regarding your new attire," she explained. "Some of the other employees have felt your colors are a bit – distracting."

Normally, I would have retreated – curled up inside myself, coiled like a mamba in some secret part of myself where not even shame or guilt can follow.

But, much to my surprise, I didn't.

I found myself stretching out, as if pleased to show her how wicked I can be – as if I were that very same carnivorous plant they thought of me, the very same monster they had already named me.

"We're going to ask you take the rest of the day off," she told me.

So, I packed my things and left the office for the day. When I walked, it felt as if a thick red weed sprouted from each of my footprints – a trail for anyone daring enough to follow.

I think I've earned my eyes for another day. Don't you?

Agnes

EMAIL FROM ZOE CROSS

Date: 06/05/2000
Time: 8:41 p.m.
From: Zoe Cross <crushedmarigolds@[omitted].com>
To: Agnes Petrella
<agnes_in_wonderland_76@[omitted].com>
Subject: Re: The Red Dress

Agnes,

I am so delighted to hear you've reclaimed your power and that you're making colossal strides toward the owner-ship of your true identity – a fearless young woman. I knew that pushing you would result in something truly glorious, but I never expected you to present yourself with such dedication and resilience.

I'm truly impressed.

I knew defying the conventions of your place of employment's dress code would be exactly the thing you needed to recognize your true worth as a person. I only wish I could have been there to witness the carnage unfold.

I look forward to discussing more tonight on Instant Messenger. I should be on around ten-thirty, if you can make it.

I hope this isn't too forward. (But, then again, I feel as though we have no more boundaries between us.) If you'd truly like to make a bold statement and embrace your new identity, go the rest of the week without wearing any underwear.

Talk to you tonight,
Zoe

INSTANT MESSAGING CONVERSATION BETWEEN AGNES AND ZOE

06/05/2000

[<crushedmarigolds> has entered the chat]
[<agnes_in_wonderland_76> has entered the chat]

10:34:02 <crushedmarigolds> Hey
10:34:09 <crushedmarigolds> How does the snake feel in her new skin?
10:34:18 <agnes_in_wonderland_76> I feel like I could burst into flames
10:34:28 <agnes_in_wonderland_76> I've never felt this way before
10:34:37 <crushedmarigolds> Didn't take much
10:34:49 <agnes_in_wonderland_76> I could've never done this without you
10:34:59 <crushedmarigolds> We're all capable of change. Sometimes it hurts
10:35:07 <agnes_in_wonderland_76> You know what I feel like?
10:35:16 <agnes_in_wonderland_76> I feel like a new constellation, scabbed in glittering black
10:35:20 <agnes_in_wonderland_76> A smear across the universe

10:35:28 <crushedmarigolds> Wait for the asteroid
to come

10:35:40 <agnes_in_wonderland_76> No. I feel like some
shapeless cosmic belt, as if the hand of some invisible
deity were cradling me in his arms

10:35:49 <agnes_in_wonderland_76> [omitted]

10:35:57 <crushedmarigolds> You know, I wasn't joking
about the underwear…

10:36:05 <agnes_in_wonderland_76> Yeah?

10:36:09 <crushedmarigolds> Yeah…

10:36:17 <agnes_in_wonderland_76> I've been thinking
about it

10:36:29 <crushedmarigolds> And?

10:36:41 <agnes_in_wonderland_76> Do you like
thinking about me not wearing any underwear?

10:36:48 <crushedmarigolds> It's a thought I don't mind

10:36:59 <agnes_in_wonderland_76> Maybe you'd like to
tell me what else is on your mind?

10:37:08 <crushedmarigolds> Can't

10:37:13 <agnes_in_wonderland_76> Why not?

10:37:19 <crushedmarigolds> It would scare you

10:37:27 <agnes_in_wonderland_76> It wouldn't

10:37:42 <crushedmarigolds> My thoughts scare me
sometimes

10:37:49 <agnes_in_wonderland_76> Whatever you're
thinking, I probably want it

10:37:58 <crushedmarigolds> Do you?

10:38:06 <agnes_in_wonderland_76> Yeah

10:38:18 <crushedmarigolds> You'd like me to tie your
hands with rope above your head and use a leather crop to
blacken both of your ass cheeks?

10:38:27 <agnes_in_wonderland_76> Yes

10:38:35 <crushedmarigolds> How about I open you up with my fingers until they slide in deep inside, soft gurgling noises clogged in the pit of your throat?

10:38:43 <agnes_in_wonderland_76> Yeah. Don't stop, baby

10:38:49 <crushedmarigolds> You going to open up for Mommy?

10:38:59 <crushedmarigolds> I push in further and you're fully open for me

10:39:08 <agnes_in_wonderland_76> It's all for you, Mommy

10:39:12 <agnes_in_wonderland_76> I'm touching myself right now

10:39:19 <agnes_in_wonderland_76> Are you?

10:39:30 <agnes_in_wonderland_76> Why did you stop?

10:39:51 <crushedmarigolds> Don't want to scare you away

10:40:01 <agnes_in_wonderland_76> You're not going to scare me, I promise

10:40:09 <crushedmarigolds> You're going to ask what I want

10:40:18 <agnes_in_wonderland_76> What's the matter with that?

10:40:29 <crushedmarigolds> The problem is I know exactly what I want, and it's something no woman could ever give me

10:40:38 <agnes_in_wonderland_76> I could try

10:40:43 <crushedmarigolds> No

10:40:49 <agnes_in_wonderland_76> You've done so much for me. I'm happy to

10:40:57 <agnes_in_wonderland_76> What is it?

10:41:05 <crushedmarigolds> I can't talk right now

10:41:13 <agnes_in_wonderland_76> Is someone there with you?

10:41:22 <crushedmarigolds> No. Nobody's here.

10:41:28 <crushedmarigolds> I have to go.

10:41:35 <crushedmarigolds> I'll talk to you later?

10:41:44 <agnes_in_wonderland_76> Yeah. I guess I'll talk to you later.

[<crushedmarigolds> has left the chat]

[<agnes_in_wonderland_76> has left the chat]

INSTANT MESSAGING CONVERSATION BETWEEN AGNES AND ZOE

06/06/2000

[<crushedmarigolds> has entered the chat]

[<agnes_in_wonderland_76> has entered the chat]

1:39:09 <agnes_in_wonderland_76> You came back

1:39:14 <crushedmarigolds> Have you been waiting this whole time?

1:39:25 <agnes_in_wonderland_76> I couldn't sleep

1:39:33 <agnes_in_wonderland_76> I had hoped you'd come back

1:39:46 <agnes_in_wonderland_76> Why did you leave?

1:39:14 <crushedmarigolds> I was scared

1:39:55 <agnes_in_wonderland_76> Scared of what?

1:40:03 <crushedmarigolds> Losing you

1:40:12 <agnes_in_wonderland_76> Why would you lose me?

1:40:20 <crushedmarigolds> Because I thought about telling you what I really wanted

1:40:29 <agnes_in_wonderland_76> I want you to tell me. I need you to tell me.

1:40:46 <crushedmarigolds> You won't be scared?

1:40:57 <agnes_in_wonderland_76> You could never scare me

1:41:05 <crushedmarigolds> I want a woman to belong to me

1:41:13 <agnes_in_wonderland_76> I want that, too

1:41:22 <crushedmarigolds> No, you don't get it

1:41:34 <agnes_in_wonderland_76> I'm trying. Just help me out

1:41:39 <crushedmarigolds> I want somebody I can take care of – in every possible way

1:41:44 <agnes_in_wonderland_76> Yes

1:41:49 <crushedmarigolds> Somebody who answers only to me, as if I were the hand of God that feeds them

1:42:03 <crushedmarigolds> Somebody who would be willing to give up their freedom so that I could command them

1:42:12 <crushedmarigolds> I would have access to their email, their bank account – every little thing that makes up a fully formed person

1:42:19 <crushedmarigolds> They would belong to me and, in return, I would take care of them the way a mother nurtures a child

1:42:28 <crushedmarigolds> They would never work another day in their life, unless they wanted to

1:42:39 <crushedmarigolds> I would do everything in my power to protect them, to care for them – as long as they willingly gave themselves to me

1:42:54 <crushedmarigolds> Are you still there?

1:43:01 <agnes_in_wonderland_76> I'm here

1:43:09 <crushedmarigolds> Are you scared?

1:43:17 <agnes_in_wonderland_76> No

1:43:26 <crushedmarigolds> You asked what I wanted

1:43:33 <agnes_in_wonderland_76> Yes, I wanted
to know

1:43:40 <crushedmarigolds> I understand if you'd rather
keep your distance for awhile

1:43:49 <agnes_in_wonderland_76> I'll do it

1:43:58 <crushedmarigolds> What?

1:44:06 <agnes_in_wonderland_76> I would give myself
entirely to you

1:44:17 <agnes_in_wonderland_76> After everything
you've done for me

1:44:27 <crushedmarigolds> You're serious?

1:44:39 <agnes_in_wonderland_76> I told you I wanted to
repay you for your kindness

1:44:44 <crushedmarigolds> No

1:44:52 <agnes_in_wonderland_76> What do you
mean "no?"

1:45:03 <crushedmarigolds> I want you to say "yes"
because it's something you want, yearn for. Not because
it's a debt you feel you need to repay

1:45:10 <agnes_in_wonderland_76> It's something I want,
believe me

1:45:19 <agnes_in_wonderland_76> If you promise to
take care of me

1:45:28 <crushedmarigolds> I would

1:45:37 <agnes_in_wonderland_76> Then, it's something
I want

1:45:49 <crushedmarigolds> You're sure you're willing to
do this?

1:45:59 <agnes_in_wonderland_76> I would do anything for you
1:46:04 <crushedmarigolds> Yes
1:46:09 <agnes_in_wonderland_76> I'm serious
1:46:18 <crushedmarigolds> If you're serious, I'll draw up a contract
1:46:22 <agnes_in_wonderland_76> Fancy
1:46:29 <crushedmarigolds> I'll send it over in a day or two
1:46:38 <agnes_in_wonderland_76> I'll be waiting for it
1:46:44 <crushedmarigolds> Talk soon?
1:46:50 <agnes_in_wonderland_76> Yeah, talk soon

[<crushedmarigolds> has left the chat]
[<agnes_in_wonderland_76> has left the chat]

EMAIL FROM ZOE CROSS

[The following is an email sent from Zoe Cross's email account to Agnes Petrella's where she tortuously details the intricacies of their proposed Master/Slave relationship. As with most other sections of text in this publication, certain areas of writing have been censored or redacted under the supervision of the Henley's Edge Police Department. These areas have been written as [omitted].]

Date: 06/07/2000
Time: 10:06 a.m.
From: Zoe Cross <crushedmarigolds@[omitted].com>
To: Agnes Petrella
<agnes_in_wonderland_76@[omitted].com>
Subject: Contract Agreement

CONTRACT AGREEMENT
between

<u>Zoe Cross</u>

and

<u>Agnes Petrella</u>

<u>Zoe Cross</u>, hereinafter referred to as "Sponsor," hereby binds this contract with <u>Agnes Petrella</u>, hereinafter referred to as "Drudge" in this Contract of Sponsorship. Said contract refers to total dominance and control of Owner in this relationship with said "Drudge" in regard to the stipulations contained herein. It is to be noted that that the official agreement was reached on the day of <u>June 7th, 2000</u>. This contract is to be a written declaration of this fact.

This contract is in no way legally binding in a court of law but is meant as an aid to better understanding of the needs, duties, and responsibilities of the Sponsor and the Drudge. Both the Sponsor and Drudge agree upon the details of this relationship, with both parties accepting and understanding the consequences of such.

[Omitted]

. . .

PURPOSE

The purpose of this instrument is to:

- State the full mutual consent of the above mentioned in regard to this relationship

- Explain the responsibilities and duties of both Sponsor and Drudge

- Explain the use of punishment

- Define all set rules and possible future rules

This contract is written to make clear the expectations of Sponsor and the consequences for failure to live up to this agreement.

The said parties, for the consideration hereinafter mentioned, hereby agree to the following:

1. The Drudge agrees to obey to the best of her ability, and to devote herself entirely to the pleasures and desires of the Sponsor. The Drudge also renounces all rights to her own pleasure, comfort, or gratification except insofar as permitted by the Sponsor.

2. The Drudge agrees to hand over the password and all subsequent details of her bank account information to the Sponsor so that the Sponsor is in full control of her accounts. The Drudge agrees to never question the Sponsor with regard to finances and fully understands that the Sponsor's full possession of her account is for her physical and mental well-being.

3. The Drudge will sleep in the nude with the air conditioning on full blast, even in winter months. This is intended to show servitude to the Sponsor and is a means by which the Drudge can make a small sacrifice in order to exhibit an unparalleled level of loyalty.

4. The Drudge will only consume food at the following times: 10 a.m., 1 p.m., and 6 p.m. This strict regimen of feeding will not only improve digestion but will keep the Drudge balanced and in good faith with the Sponsor.

5. The Drudge will confer with the Sponsor before making any large purchases as the Sponsor holds the account information for the Drudge.

6. The Sponsor accepts full responsibility of the Drudge. This includes but is not limited to: the Drudge's survival, health, physical well-being, and mental well-being. The Drudge accepts full responsibility for informing the Sponsor of any real or perceived dangers or safety concerns, but also agrees that the Sponsor's decision will be final regarding these issues.

7. The Drudge agrees and understands that any infractions of this contract, or any act the Drudge commits which displeases the Sponsor, will result in punishment.

8. This agreement may not be assigned by either party to any third party.

9. This agreement may be amended in writing at the Sponsor's behest and will require compliance from both parties

[Omitted]

This contract is valid from the day the Drudge replies to this email with "Accepted, understood, and agreed to" and is effective for all time unless terminated by the Sponsor.

EMAIL FROM AGNES PETRELLA

Date: 06/07/2000
Time: 12:05 p.m.
From: Agnes Petrella <agnes_in_wonderland_76@[omitted].com>
To: Zoe Cross <crushedmarigolds@[omitted].com>
Subject: Re: Contract Agreement

> Accepted, understood, and agreed to.
> Signed,
> Agnes Petrella

PART THREE
A SALAMANDER FROM THE PARK

EMAIL FROM ZOE CROSS

Date: 06/08/2000
Time: 6:49 a.m.
From: Zoe Cross <crushedmarigolds@[omitted].com>
To: Agnes Petrella
<agnes_in_wonderland_76@[omitted].com>
Subject: A Drudge's Duties

Good morning Drudge,

I trust you slept well.

I imagine you're getting ready to leave for work, and that's precisely why I'm emailing you.

I have another task for you. Something that will undoubtedly make you uncomfortable. Then again, aren't those the moments when we change the most – when we're uncomfortable?

I'd like you to go into the communal bathroom at work

and leave your undergarments in the stall for someone to find. Perhaps a pair embellished with lace, or maybe a pair you've yet to wash.

Regardless of the pair you choose, I want the undergarment deserted in a conspicuous place – where someone can and will find it.

I trust you will complete this task in as expeditious a manner as possible and will reply to this message with "Done" when you have properly executed the assignment.

What have you done today to deserve your eyes?

Yours,

Sponsor

EMAIL FROM AGNES PETRELLA

Date: 06/08/2000
Time: 9:09 a.m.
From: Agnes Petrella <agnes_in_wonderland_76@[omitted].com>
To: Zoe Cross <crushedmarigolds@[omitted].com>
Subject: Re: A Drudge's Duties

    Done.
    Signed,
    Agnes Petrella

EMAIL FROM AGNES PETRELLA

Date: 06/08/2000
Time: 2:17 p.m.

From: Agnes Petrella <agnes_in_wonderland_76@[omit-ted].com>
To: Zoe Cross <crushedmarigolds@[omitted].com>
Subject: Re: A Drudge's Duties

Well, it finally happened.

I was asked to leave today. Only this time, for good.

I crept into the ladies' washroom when I was certain it was empty, skirted into one of the empty stalls, and slid off the pair of underwear I wore to work today. It was a dark cherry color, the edges frilled with lace as finely woven as a spider's web.

When I had fully removed the underwear, wrenching it off from around my shoes, I wrapped the garment around the toilet seat's handlebar. I stepped back, admiring the finesse of my craftsmanship. The underwear dangled there obscenely as if it were human viscera on display – a juice-less organ or a dried-out intestine to be marveled at.

After I was satisfied with my work, I crawled out of the empty stall. But just as I was leaving, one of the other secretaries greeted me at the washroom door. She made a friendly comment, excusing herself as she almost bumped into me. Then, I watched her eyes drift to the pair of undergarments hanging from the handlebar in the empty stall.

She looked at me strangely, as if searching me for an explanation. When she could find none, she made her way into one of the other stalls and shut the door.

I sneaked back to my desk and waited for the moment when it would happen – the moment when I would be once again asked to visit my superior's office. Only this time, I decided I would accept my fate with the same dignity of a virgin martyr being led to public execution.

Finally, the time came.

"She'd like to see you in her office," one of the other younger secretaries told me while keeping their distance, as if I carried some infectious disease and they might be dismissed as well if they came too close to me.

The meeting was brief. Just as I had expected. A simple, "You're dismissed" and a few papers to sign.

I didn't feel anything when I was asked to pack my things. I thought I might feel a pinch in the center of my chest, a faucet leaking behind my eyes. But, no. Nothing.

It's not that I felt empty. I think all of us feel empty most of the time and we merely pretend to fill the vacuum with laughter, crying, apologies – anything to make us feel human.

I think I felt like what an astronaut feels like when they hurdle toward earth in a tiny prison chamber, flames eating away at their vessel as they enter our atmosphere.

There's a reason objects burn up when they fall to earth like gruesome angels – a reason other than the obvious one. Asteroids the size of armored cars narrow to mere pebbles in a matter of seconds. It's because the planet is a carnivore and just wants to be fed. People want that as well. People like to eat other people.

I spent so many years forgetting I had teeth, too.

So, I packed my things up and hurried out of the office, swiping the underwear from the washroom stall before I forgot. I stepped out onto the street, daylight running its fingers through my hair as if it were a fire. That's when I thought of you.

I know you'll take care of me.

You won't eat me. No matter how much you enjoy the way I taste.

EMAIL FROM ZOE CROSS

Date: 06/08/2000
Time: 4:13 p.m.
From: Zoe Cross <crushedmarigolds@[omitted].com>
To: Agnes Petrella
<agnes_in_wonderland_76@[omitted].com>
Subject: Re: A Drudge's Duties

Drudge,

I'm devastated to learn of your recent dismissal. But I'm delighted to know you don't view this slight impediment as a major setback.

In truth, I was considering reaching out to you and explaining that you no longer need to work when you're under my care. I assured you that I will take care of you and I certainly do not intend to neglect my side of our agreement.

We can discuss this further tonight on Instant Messenger. I'll be on at ten o'clock. I expect to see you there.

Signed,

Sponsor

INSTANT MESSAGING CONVERSATION BETWEEN AGNES AND ZOE

06/08/2000

[<crushedmarigolds> has entered the chat]
[<agnes_in_wonderland_76> has entered the chat]

10:01:04 <agnes_in_wonderland_76> Hi
10:01:08 <crushedmarigolds> You're late
10:01:14 <agnes_in_wonderland_76> I'm sorry
10:01:20 <crushedmarigolds> Sorry what?
10:01:31 <agnes_in_wonderland_76> Sorry, Sponsor
10:01:43 <crushedmarigolds> That's a good Drudge
10:01:52 <crushedmarigolds> You understand the penance for being late?
10:02:03 <agnes_in_wonderland_76> Yes, Sponsor
10:02:14 <crushedmarigolds> You're to hold your breath for a minute
10:02:22 <agnes_in_wonderland_76> Yes, Sponsor
10:02:34 <crushedmarigolds> Deep breath
10:02:39 <crushedmarigolds> Starting now
10:02:45 <crushedmarigolds> Don't breathe
10:02:52 <crushedmarigolds> Not yet
10:03:05 <crushedmarigolds> Keep it held
10:03:14 <crushedmarigolds> Not done yet
10:03:22 <crushedmarigolds> Almost there
10:03:29 <crushedmarigolds> Almost
10:03:35 <crushedmarigolds> Now
10:03:39 <crushedmarigolds> Breathe
10:03:49 <crushedmarigolds> What do you say?
10:03:55 <agnes_in_wonderland_76> Thank you, Sponsor

10:04:07 <crushedmarigolds> That's a good girl

10:04:15 <crushedmarigolds> Now, the matter of your allowance...

10:04:22 <agnes_in_wonderland_76> Allowance?

10:04:31 <crushedmarigolds> Don't you think that's fair?

10:04:44 <agnes_in_wonderland_76> Yes. I guess so...

10:04:50 <agnes_in_wonderland_76> That's very generous of you

10:05:01 <crushedmarigolds> I'll deposit fifteen hundred dollars in your account on the first of every month

10:05:11 <agnes_in_wonderland_76> Fifteen hundred?!!

10:05:22 <crushedmarigolds> A fair amount?

10:05:29 <agnes_in_wonderland_76> I would say so.

10:05:33 <agnes_in_wonderland_76> It's too generous

10:05:41 <crushedmarigolds> You know Mommy wants to take care of her girl

10:05:55 <agnes_in_wonderland_76> Yes. I know

10:06:03 <crushedmarigolds> Is there anything you want?

10:06:11 <agnes_in_wonderland_76> Anything I want?

10:06:19 <crushedmarigolds> If you could have anything

10:06:29 <crushedmarigolds> Name it

10:06:38 <agnes_in_wonderland_76> I want to see you in person

10:06:44 <agnes_in_wonderland_76> I want to be able to touch you

10:06:55 <agnes_in_wonderland_76> To know you're real

10:07:04 <crushedmarigolds> Aren't I real enough for you already?

10:07:12 <agnes_in_wonderland_76> You're just a blinking cursor to me right now

10:07:20 <agnes_in_wonderland_76> I want to know you're real

10:07:31 <agnes_in_wonderland_76> To feel your blood pumping, the heartbeat in your hands

10:07:40 <crushedmarigolds> I've already done so much to prove to you I'm real

10:07:51 <agnes_in_wonderland_76> I suppose I just can't believe a person as good as you exists

10:08:03 <agnes_in_wonderland_76> Don't you want us to be together?

10:08:10 <crushedmarigolds> Of course I do

10:08:21 <crushedmarigolds> How could you ask me that?

10:08:30 <agnes_in_wonderland_76> Then, why can't we?

10:08:44 <crushedmarigolds> It's not that I don't want to

10:08:52 <crushedmarigolds> We're not ready yet

10:09:01 <agnes_in_wonderland_76> Will we be?

10:09:09 <crushedmarigolds> Some day

10:09:17 <crushedmarigolds> Just not today

10:09:24 <agnes_in_wonderland_76> You asked me if there's something I want

10:09:29 <crushedmarigolds> Yes

10:09:34 <agnes_in_wonderland_76> More than anything in the world

10:09:43 <crushedmarigolds> Tell me

10:09:55 <agnes_in_wonderland_76> I want a baby

10:10:02 <crushedmarigolds> Yes

10:10:15 <agnes_in_wonderland_76> I want life to carry inside me

10:10:25 <agnes_in_wonderland_76> That's what I've wanted more than anything else

10:10:33 <agnes_in_wonderland_76> To be a mother

10:10:56 <agnes_in_wonderland_76> You still there?

10:11:03 <crushedmarigolds> I wish I could give you that

10:11:09 <crushedmarigolds> I would if I could
10:11:17 <agnes_in_wonderland_76> I know you would
10:11:28 <crushedmarigolds> I can't stay
10:11:37 <agnes_in_wonderland_76> You have to leave already?
10:11:48 <crushedmarigolds> We'll talk tomorrow?
10:11:55 <agnes_in_wonderland_76> Always

[<crushedmarigolds> has left the chat]
[<agnes_in_wonderland_76> has left the chat]

EMAIL FROM ZOE CROSS

Date: 06/10/2000
Time: 2:04 a.m.
From: Zoe Cross <crushedmarigolds@[omitted].com>
To: Agnes Petrella
<agnes_in_wonderland_76@[omitted].com>
Subject: A Salamander from the Park

I thought of something before going to bed tonight. I've been thinking a lot about what you said – how you want to carry life, how you want something to care for.

I think there's a way for us both to get what we want.

I want you to visit a park near your apartment. I checked on the map and I see that there's a place called White Memorial not far from where you live.

I want you to go there and comb the grounds for a salamander.

A wet, oily little thing – probably could contentedly fit inside the palm of your hand.

You can usually find them in moist areas. They prefer marshlands – freshwater creeks or brooks. I've read they typically hide under rocks, their little bodies seeking out damp, cool places.

I want you to take the salamander from where you find it and stuff it inside your pocket. Keep it tucked there so that it's comfortable. I want you to carry it with you all day. No matter where you go. If it suffocates in there, I want you to return to the park and find another one.

I want you to do this all day until sunset.

Then, when twilight devours color from the sky, I want you to take the salamander to a place outdoors where nobody can find you. I want you to find a large rock and smash it against the small creature until it stops moving.

You probably didn't know the salamander is a symbol of rebirth in many cultures – a sign of change, transformation, and growth.

Don't you wish to be reborn too?

After all, what have you done today to deserve your eyes?

Signed,

Sponsor

EMAIL FROM AGNES PETRELLA

Date: 06/10/2000
Time: 8:37 a.m.
From: Agnes Petrella <agnes_in_wonderland_76@[omitted].com>
To: Zoe Cross <crushedmarigolds@[omitted].com>
Subject: Re: A Salamander from the Park

Sponsor,

I've read your email several times now and I'm uncertain where to begin.

You know I would never question you or do anything to challenge your judgement. But I don't think I could go through with it.

I could never hurt a living thing.

Will you please reconsider and give me another task?

I'll do anything else. I swear it.

Signed,

Drudge

EMAIL FROM ZOE CROSS

Date: 06/10/2000
Time: 9:49 a.m.
From: Zoe Cross <crushedmarigolds@[omitted].com>
To: Agnes Petrella
<agnes_in_wonderland_76@[omitted].com>
Subject: Re: A Salamander from the Park

A Drudge does not question their Sponsor. A Drudge obeys no matter what.

EMAIL FROM AGNES PETRELLA

Date: 06/10/2000
Time: 10:11 p.m.
From: Agnes Petrella <agnes_in_wonderland_76@[omitted].com>

Zoe Cross <crushedmarigolds@[omitted].com>
Re: A Salamander from the Park

I did what you asked me to.

I didn't take pictures of any of it, so my account of everything will have to suffice.

I got in my car and took a drive out to the park this afternoon. The one you mentioned in your email. There was a huge iron gate that greeted me when I arrived, miniature stone gargoyles flanking either side that seemed to regard me as if incredulous, as if they were about to ask me what I was doing there. At the time, I remember thinking how wonderful it might be if one day we had a place with a gate guarded by little stone beasts with ferocious jaws – little creatures that would belong to us and no one else.

So, after I paid the attendant, I drove through the gate and began to meander down a narrow corridor lined with giant Sycamores. I remember thinking, "What am I doing?"

"I shouldn't be here."

"I shouldn't be doing this."

"This is wrong."

But, with every barbed thought, I sensed my feet pushed down harder on the accelerator as if I were gleefully headed toward doom, as if I had caught a glimpse of Hell for the first time and needed to marvel further at its vast wealth of wonders.

I parked my car under a tree and headed for the pond I saw in the distance. There were a few children playing with their parents in the field beside the parking lot, but they didn't seem to notice me.

Creeping down the narrow causeway, I arrived at the pond. The water was still, lilies the size of dinner plates floating by. I started to skirt around the edges of the pond, my head craning beneath the underbrush beside the path. I located some small rocks on the water's shore, flipping them over and finding nothing.

Then, after an hour or so of searching, I noticed a small, dark shape stirring in the grass further up ahead near the water's edge. I looked closer and it was then I found what I was looking for – a salamander, the size of a housekey and practically just as flat. Its tail was slippery wet, and its skin glinted in the sunlight as I spooned it from the ground to hold in my hand.

There's something Godlike about holding something so small – something that solely depends on your kindness, your generosity. I had never thought about hurting something before. Until now. I imagined what it might feel like. I imagined closing my hand to make a fist until its tiny body was squished, its innards squeezed out like toothpaste from its mouth open in a muted scream.

Before I allowed myself to get too carried away with the thought, I shoved the little creature inside my pocket. I named him Albert and promised I would treat him with crickets if he behaved. He wouldn't know the difference if I didn't, and I knew he wouldn't call me a liar.

So, as promised, I carried him with me all day, my eyes glancing at my wristwatch every minute or so as if I were anticipating my own execution at twilight. Finally, the moment I had been dreading arrived – all light vacuumed from the sky.

So, I returned to the park after dusk and I took the little creature to a small grove of trees just beyond the parking lot. I sprawled him out along a moss-covered rock, and I searched for a rock nearby. When I finally located one – about the size of a bowling ball – I approached Albert with a wordless apology. He remained perfectly still, as if comfortable in my presence and foolishly thinking I would never do anything to harm him.

Before another moment of hesitation, I brought down the rock and slammed it against him. I heard a vulgar, wet thud. I looked down and saw the poor, pathetic creature – flattened – and crumpled like windblown paper against the rock's underside. After peeling his little body from the rock, he flopped to the ground and twitched gently before I saw his tiny legs stop from trembling.

The whole forest seemed to fall quiet, as if in mourning for the small creature.

So, I found a spot beneath a tree and dug a small hole in the dirt. I ladled his little body from the ground and said a prayer before tossing him in the tiny pit I had opened.

I stood there at his grave for what felt like hours. Then, when darkness leeched through the trees, I packed my things, headed for my car, and drove back home.

As I sit here at my computer, with dirt beneath my fingernails, I wonder why I did this, why I ever agreed to let you tell me what to do.

I never thought I would ever do something as monstrous, as wicked as this.

That poor creature didn't deserve to die, and I did it just to please you.

What else will I do to make you happy?

What else will I do before you finally take my eyes from me, as you've been promising?

You and I are better off without each other.

If we stay together, we'll only hurt one another.

I've been thinking about that a lot lately. Especially about a Sumatran short-eared rabbit. Have you ever seen one? It's a type of rabbit only found in Indonesia. Considered very rare. Endangered, in fact. They had one at the zoo I used to go to when I was in college. I used to skip my French class and instead take a walk to the zoo - stroll through the gardens, look at the orangutans and the lemurs, and the sloths and the pandas.

But I always found myself drawn to a small glass case framed on the pathway leading to the anteater exhibit. A small glass case with a female Sumatran short-eared rabbit inside. She'd squat in her little cage, her tiny hands cupping the bits of tropical fruit they'd give her. Her fur – warm chestnut with dark brown stripes. She was about as big as your hand. Maybe a little bit bigger.

I found out she was pregnant.

And the zookeepers were taking bets when she'd finally deliver the litter.

So, I kept checking back every day – ignoring my French homework and instead sprinting to the zoo to see if the rabbit had her babies yet.

And finally, one day, when I was there, she was laying on her side and it started to happen. Squeezing out of her was this tiny, pink clump of tissue – glistening wet. She labored for probably twenty minutes before the little thing pushed itself out of her, its limbs shiny and rubbery. And as it lay there, twitching in the agony of what it feels like to first become a living thing, she pressed her snout against it and inhaled its scent.

She did this a few times, pushing herself against the infant harder each time as if testing its comfort. And finally, as she started to give birth to the next baby, she wrapped her mouth around the rabbit she had just delivered and started devouring it.

I just stood there, watching helplessly as the mother rabbit ate her child – bits of tissue and blood smearing against her gnarled fur.

I didn't watch the rest of the carnage.

I walked back to my dorm, not remembering how I got there when I finally arrived. I went back to the zoo a month or so later and one of the zookeepers told me that the mother ate the other baby as well – not long after she ate the first one.

He said the baby rabbit was sick and wouldn't have survived even if they intervened in time. Said this happens all the time in the wild because a carcass will usually draw predators to the den. He said it was probably for the best.

Just like this decision is for the best.

This is where it stops.

I've made the decision to not go forward with our contract. I will not be answering any more of your emails, nor will I be financially engaging with you in any way.

I will be going to my bank tomorrow and wiring the money back into your account. I will also be closing my accounts and doing my banking elsewhere so that you no longer have access to my finances.

I'm petitioning you to please void our current contract as I refuse to move forward with any of your tasks.

I'm better off without you.

Signed,

Agnes

EMAIL FROM ZOE CROSS

Date: 06/10/2000
Time: 11:39 p.m.
From: Zoe Cross <crushedmarigolds@[omitted].com>
To: Agnes Petrella
<agnes_in_wonderland_76@[omitted].com>
Subject: Contract Voided

Agnes,

I'm disheartened to hear of your decision to void our current contract; however, I understand your cause for doing so.

I am truly sorry that I pushed you well beyond your limit. That was never my intention.

I think we both wanted different things out of this relationship and we're coming to the realization that it simply isn't a good fit.

I honor your decision and this email is sent as a voidance of our current contract.

I wish you nothing but health and prosperity in all your future endeavors. I am always here if you need anything.

Best regards,

Zoe

PART FOUR

AN EGG BEFORE IT CRACKS

EMAIL FROM AGNES PETRELLA

Date: 07/28/2000
Time: 10:01 p.m.
From: Agnes Petrella <agnes_in_wonderland_76@[omitted].com>
To: Zoe Cross <crushedmarigolds@[omitted].com>
Subject: An Apology I Owe You

Hey,

I understand if you'd rather not talk to me after the way I left things over a month ago. But I've been thinking so much about you lately.

It probably doesn't help that I have the apple peeler pinned to my kitchen wall. There were so many times I had contemplated whether or not I should just send it to you with a note telling you how sorry I am.

But I worried you might toss out the box before you even opened it.

Not that you don't have a right to be mad. You are well within reason to not want to talk to me, or to simply tell me to fuck off. Of course, I hope you don't do those things. But what I'm trying to say is that I understand if that's how you feel. I did something to you I'll never forgive myself for as long as I live. After all your consideration, your kindness – to have it thrown back in your face with the same disregard that people might consider when contemplating weekly trash disposal. There's no worse insult I can think of.

It was never my intention to hurt you. I don't really think I'm better off without you. I should've never said that. Sometimes we say or do things to people we love because we know it will hurt them.

Besides, what I had done nearly isn't as horrible as what some other people have done.

For God's sake, there are people who impale baby birds with toothpicks. Or people who pour bleach inside cats' ears.

I don't know about you but hearing about the terrible things other people have done have always made me feel better about the things I've done.

I remember watching a TV interview with a teenager who had crucified his little brother. You probably heard about it. He called his brother "The Little Christ" because his parents endlessly doted on the child.

Anyway, they had him in handcuffs on TV – dressed in an orange jumpsuit, chatting with a reporter. And he starts talking about how he did it.

He waits until his parents go to sleep one night, and he

creeps into the nursery, spooning his baby brother from his cradle into his arms. The child makes little mewling noises like a kitten, but he keeps a blanket over his mouth to muffle the sounds. After he's finished loading up the car with the supplies he needs, he ferries the Little Christ from the house to the backseat of his station-wagon. He shifts the car into gear and before long he's on the road, hurtling down the highway as if he were bound for the Promised Land, Shangri-La – anywhere but here.

He thinks about how he should do it first. Should he just kill him and get it over with? Or should he take his time and make it as perfect as possible?

So, after driving for about half an hour, they arrive at the rock quarry on the outskirts of town. He drives to the small ledge overlooking the nearby park where those evangelists built a giant crucifix out of unused pine. So, he pulls the Little Christ out of the car seat and hauls him up toward the cross. The crucifix isn't very large. Maybe six feet tall at most. So, he positions the Little Christ against it – splaying his limbs out against the wood. The child struggles a little. He looks around confused, bands of drool collecting in the corners of his little mouth.

It's now or never, he thinks to himself.

So, he reaches inside the rucksack he's brought with him and he pulls out a hammer and a small nail. He presses the Little Christ's hand against the arm of the cross and that's when he starts to cry, as if the child somehow realizes what he's about to do. Whether he knows his fate before it happens or not, it soon becomes clear to him when he swings the hammer down and smashes the nail through the palm of his little hand. He shrieks as if he were a wounded animal. It sounds almost – inhuman. Pitiful.

Like the final pathetic cry of a dying species – a breed on the verge of being swallowed by oblivion.

He can't stop now.

He's already gone too far.

Blood's leaking from the hole he's opened in the Little Christ's hand. So, he holds him up to keep him from falling and he rummages through his rucksack again until he finds another nail. He stretches his other hand along the other arm of the cross and smashes the hammer down until the nail disappears in a bubble of blood. He removes his hands from him, and he lets the child dangle there, his palms tearing gently under the weight of being held up by the small nails. The Little Christ hangs there, screaming until hoarse – like some sacred offering for an ancient deity. The noise is almost unbearable.

But he's not finished yet.

So, he pulls out a small hunter's knife his father had given him for his twelfth birthday. He slices the baby's belly open until a thin line of blood creeps from the tiny hole he had opened there. It's finished. He doesn't have a crown of thorns to complete the likeness, but he thinks the Little Christ doesn't deserve one.

Once he's finished arranging the child on the cross, braiding ropes around his arms to keep him from falling, he returns to the car to retrieve his paint supplies. He sets his easel up in a small area not far from the cross and as the dawn breaks, he begins to work on his painting. It's not long before the Little Christ's screams dim until they're soundless, his head lowering as if in prayer. He doesn't bother to check. But he knows he's dead.

He doesn't remember what happens next until he sees

flashing lights – red and blue – idling toward his car on the quarry's ledge.

The interviewer asks the teenager, "If you could see your baby brother again, what would you say to him?"

The teenager inhales, as if thinking deeply. Then, quite matter-of-factly, he stares straight ahead at the interview with a blank expression and says one word: "Nothing."

I could never dream of being a monster like that.

Neither of us are monsters.

Don't we deserve a second chance?

I hope you'll accept this email as my apology and – if you're willing, of course – I hope you'll accept me as your Drudge once more to be faithful to you and to give myself entirely to you.

I'll be waiting for your email.

Love,

Agnes

EMAIL FROM AGNES PETRELLA

Date: 07/30/2000
Time: 11:37 p.m.
From: Agnes Petrella <agnes_in_wonderland_76@[omit-ted].com>
To: Zoe Cross <crushedmarigolds@[omitted].com>
Subject: Re: An Apology I Owe You

Please write back. I promise to dedicate myself entirely to you.

I'm not better off without you.

I wrote you that story about "The Little Christ"

because I wanted to show you there are worse people in the world. We don't belong in their company. We belong together. I know we do.

Agnes

EMAIL FROM ZOE CROSS

Date: 07/31/2000
Time: 8:32 p.m.
From: Zoe Cross <crushedmarigolds@[omitted].com>
To: Agnes Petrella
<agnes_in_wonderland_76@[omitted].com>
Subject: Re: An Apology I Owe You

Agnes,

I'm sorry if I've been keeping you on edge the past few days since you sent your first email. I've been unexpectedly busy at work and I've been trying my best to stay afloat while juggling so many different projects.

I, of course, accept your apology. I was hoping you would eventually reach out as I've been thinking of you a lot lately as well.

I agree to resuming our contract and moving forward with your proposal. I don't necessarily think we need to agree to the contract again as we both understand the consequences of going against what the document stipulates.

However, I do want it known that I require full obedience and honesty if this relationship is to thrive. Any disloyalty, deceit, or noncompliance will be met with a termination of the contract and we will once again go our separate ways.

I'll be on Instant Messenger tomorrow night at 11. We can discuss more then.

Yours,

Zoe

INSTANT MESSAGING CONVERSATION BETWEEN AGNES AND ZOE

07/31/2000

[<crushedmarigolds> has entered the chat]
[<agnes_in_wonderland_76> has entered the chat]

11:00:32 <crushedmarigolds> Hey

11:00:49 <crushedmarigolds> Right on time

11:00:57 <agnes_in_wonderland_76> I told you things would be different now

11:01:05 <crushedmarigolds> Yes. I'm glad.

11:01:12 <crushedmarigolds> Glad you're here

11:01:19 <crushedmarigolds> Glad you came back

11:01:25 <agnes_in_wonderland_76> I could never stay away from you

11:01:37 <agnes_in_wonderland_76> You're the only person in my life who hasn't asked me to leave

11:01:46 <crushedmarigolds> Why would I do that?

11:01:58 <agnes_in_wonderland_76> When I was little, I thought if people hurt you, it meant that they loved you

11:02:04 <crushedmarigolds> What made you think that?

11:02:19 <agnes_in_wonderland_76> My parents worked

a lot when I was younger, and they asked my aunt to look after me while they were out.

11:02:38 <agnes_in_wonderland_76> My aunt used to play a game with me to keep me quiet, keep me out of the way. She would make me hold an egg and send me into a locked broom closet.

11:02:54 <agnes_in_wonderland_76> She used to make me stand in there, holding the egg for hours on end. When it was time to come out, she used to inspect the egg and make sure it hadn't cracked.

11:02:13 <agnes_in_wonderland_76> If it had cracked, she used to make me eat it. Every last drop. Even the shell.

11:02:29 <agnes_in_wonderland_76> I'd stand there crying, egg smeared all over my face. And she'd say, "I only do this because there are people out there who will do far worse to you."

11:02:38 <agnes_in_wonderland_76> I guess that's what makes people do horrible things – they think whatever they're doing isn't nearly as bad as what somebody else will do

11:02:50 <crushedmarigolds> I would never do anything horrible to you

11:03:01 <agnes_in_wonderland_76> I know you wouldn't

11:03:12 <crushedmarigolds> Everything I've asked of you, I've made you do – it's been from a place of love

11:03:19 <agnes_in_wonderland_76> I know it has

11:03:28 <agnes_in_wonderland_76> That's why I came back

11:03:39 <agnes_in_wonderland_76> Someone else would do far worse things to me

11:03:48 <crushedmarigolds> I would never let that happen

11:03:56 <crushedmarigolds> We made an arrangement. Remember?

11:04:03 <agnes_in_wonderland_76> Yes

11:04:11 <agnes_in_wonderland_76> Do you ever worry you'll hurt me?

11:04:16 <crushedmarigolds> Sometimes

11:04:22 <crushedmarigolds> I once dreamt about killing you

11:04:39 <crushedmarigolds> It wasn't one of those dreams you wake up from in a cold sweat, heart pumping like an engine – feeling like you've just run headfirst into a concrete wall. Skull cracked open and juices leaking everywhere.

11:05:03 <crushedmarigolds> And it definitely wasn't one of those dreams where you wake up and find the place between your legs wetting, thighs clenching at the mere reminder of the memory. Wasn't even a dream you remember when you first wake up. It was something that came to me over time, slowly crawling around inside my head like a beetle – circling some invisible drain fixed inside there and making its way down into the sludge where memories collect.

11:05:32 <crushedmarigolds> In the dream, you didn't speak.

11:05:37 <crushedmarigolds> You couldn't.

11:05:59 <crushedmarigolds> In the way that all dreams give you supernatural powers – abilities beyond comprehension or even logic – I was able to make you mute. Mouth could open, but no sound could come out. When I asked you why you couldn't speak, you gestured to my hand. It was then that I realized I had ripped out your tongue and it wiggled between my fingers like a rubbery slice of uncooked meat.

11:06:09 <crushedmarigolds> You had showed up on my front porch, suitcase in hand.

11:06:34 <crushedmarigolds> I asked you what you're doing here. You tell me you have nowhere else to go.

11:07:04 <crushedmarigolds> Before I can challenge you again, there's a horrible explosion outside. I go to the window to look and I'm greeted by a desolate wasteland. The front lawn – once a beautiful emerald carpet – now merely rusted brown and the edges burning. In the distance, a giant mushroom cloud rises into sight. The light around us dims as if the hand of God had drawn a dark curtain over the world. The windows to the house explode, a glittering hailstorm of glass flutters around us like a snow squall.

11:07:35 <crushedmarigolds> I suddenly realize you're gone, and it's then I'm approached by a nurse and she tells me that you're upstairs waiting for me.

11:07:45 <crushedmarigolds> "Upstairs?" I say.

11:08:09 <crushedmarigolds> So, I walk up the stairs to the master bedroom and somehow, I already have the key to unlock the door. I open it and it's not the master bedroom, but a giant hospital room instead. It looks like a place where they do experiments – crimes against nature – like arranging the head of a hamster on the body of a Burmese python. Something atrocious like that.

11:08:44 <crushedmarigolds> So, I inch further into the room and I see you in the hospital bed. Only difference is all your skin has been burned off. Your arms and legs – they look like thin tubes of blood sausage with the transparent casing still on them. Your face – half-melted and dripping like the wax from a candle. Your skin – shining from the radiation and so transparent that I can practically see myself in the reflection. You look so strange and yet – so mesmerizing.

11:08:58 <crushedmarigolds> Tubes and wires are connected to your fingers, snaking in and out of your mouth and nostrils. A desperate effort to keep you alive any way possible. Keep you permanently living in your agony.

11:10:08 <crushedmarigolds> I inch closer toward the bed to look at you and for some reason, I savor the moment – I savor the sight of you in pain, your eyes pleading with me to end your suffering. I think to myself, "if I were an ice pick, I'd scramble your brain like a plate of eggs." I think to myself, "if I were a black hole, I'd swallow you and shit you out in tiny pieces." I think to myself, "if I were a tomahawk, I'd split you right down the middle like a rotten piece of fruit." I'd do anything I could to erase you – smear you against the world the way a boot wipes off a squished worm on a scraper.

11:10:31 <crushedmarigolds> You motion for me to lean closer. So, I do. You can't speak, but I see your lips moving with muted words.

11:10:49 <crushedmarigolds> And you mouth the words to me – "Kill me," you say. Over and over again. "Kill me." "KILL ME."

11:10:59 <crushedmarigolds> "With what?" I ask.

11:11:52 <crushedmarigolds> Your eyes merely wander to the machine keeping you alive beside your bed. I follow your eyes and it's then I see the plug in the wall. I don't hesitate at all. One yank and it's decided. The line flattens on the screen. Doctors and nurses, their faces hidden behind surgical masks, rush into the room and examine you. They don't do much. Merely shut your eyelids before passing a white sheet over your face. Then, they turn to me.

11:12:09 <crushedmarigolds> "You have to take her place now," they say to me.

11:12:20 <crushedmarigolds> "But, I'm not sick," I say. "Look at me. I'm fine."

11:12:43 <crushedmarigolds> Then, I look down and I realize my skin has been burned off too – shining tissue blistered red staring back at me in my skin's reflection. It's not long before I take your place - reclining in the bed, machines keeping me alive.

11:13:03 <crushedmarigolds> Only this time, there's nobody around to pull the plug for me.

11:13:45 <crushedmarigolds> Are you still there?

11:13:58 <agnes_in_wonderland_76> Yeah, I'm here

11:14:09 <crushedmarigolds> Dreams can tell us things

11:14:13 <agnes_in_wonderland_76> What did that dream tell you?

11:14:23 <crushedmarigolds> How I would never want to hurt you

11:14:44 <agnes_in_wonderland_76> Yes

11:14:49 <crushedmarigolds> Also how much I love you

11:14:59 <agnes_in_wonderland_76> Love?

11:15:07 <crushedmarigolds> Does that word scare you?

11:15:09 <agnes_in_wonderland_76> No, I like it. It sounds nice.

11:15:17 <crushedmarigolds> I can't stay on. Early workday tomorrow

11:15:28 <agnes_in_wonderland_76> You'll email me?

11:15:38 <crushedmarigolds> Why wouldn't I?
11:15:44 <agnes_in_wonderland_76> Good.
11:15:49 <agnes_in_wonderland_76> I love you
11:15:55 <crushedmarigolds> Love you

[<crushedmarigolds> has left the chat]
[<agnes_in_wonderland_76> has left the chat]

EMAIL FROM AGNES PETRELLA

Date: 08/01/2000
Time: 10:09 a.m.
From: Agnes Petrella <agnes_in_wonderland_76@[omitted].com>
To: Zoe Cross <crushedmarigolds@[omitted].com>
Subject: I've been thinking…

I've been thinking a lot about our conversation the other night, and I don't want to leave any opportunity for vagueness.

I promised myself I would live unapologetically and damn anybody who finds it offensive.

I need to be as candid with you as I can possibly be. I, at the very least, owe you my honesty.

I want us to have a baby.

I know what you're thinking. I know you probably think I'm crazy, but I've been thinking about this for quite some time and I think it's only natural for the two of us to create life together.

We love one another, don't we?

We belong together.

I want to carry your life in me.

I, of course, haven't considered the details. But all I know is I want to make this happen between us. I *need* to make this happen.

What do you think?

EMAIL FROM ZOE CROSS

Date: 08/01/2000
Time: 5:12 p.m.
From: Zoe Cross <crushedmarigolds@[omitted].com>
To: Agnes Petrella
<agnes_in_wonderland_76@[omitted].com>
Subject: Re: I've been thinking…

Agnes,

I've been thinking about your email all day.

I don't quite know how to respond, and I certainly hope I don't come across as uncaring given the brevity of this email I'm writing.

Of course, I love you. Of course, I would want to have a child with you.

But it's just not possible right now. I don't know if it ever will be, but I know for certain that it's something I can't accept ownership of at the moment.

I so desperately wish I could give you exactly what you desire.

I've been thinking, too – thinking of ways we both can get what we want.

I think I've come up with a solution, but I'm apprehensive to share my idea over email. I was hoping we could chat on Instant Messenger again tonight so I can share with you my idea.

Don't worry, my love. The agony of uncertainty won't last for long.

Zoe

INSTANT MESSAGING CONVERSATION BETWEEN AGNES AND ZOE

08/01/2000

[<crushedmarigolds> has entered the chat]
[<agnes_in_wonderland_76> has entered the chat]

10:32:02 <crushedmarigolds> Hey
10:32:09 <agnes_in_wonderland_76> Hey
10:32:18 <crushedmarigolds> You're not upset, are you?
10:32:29 <agnes_in_wonderland_76> I'm bracing myself for the worst
10:32:34 <crushedmarigolds> And why's that?
10:32:41 <agnes_in_wonderland_76> You don't want to have a baby with me
10:32:54 <crushedmarigolds> That's not true
10:33:04 <crushedmarigolds> You know that's not true
10:33:12 <crushedmarigolds> I'd give anything to be able to give you exactly what you want
10:33:23 <crushedmarigolds> It's just not possible right now
10:33:35 <agnes_in_wonderland_76> I know
10:33:42 <crushedmarigolds> But, there's something you can do

10:33:53 <crushedmarigolds> If you're serious about wanting to carry life inside you

10:33:59 <agnes_in_wonderland_76> Yes

10:34:13 <crushedmarigolds> You're certain you're serious?

10:34:24 <agnes_in_wonderland_76> I want it more than anything

10:34:13 <crushedmarigolds> Then, you have to get sick

10:34:25 <agnes_in_wonderland_76> Get sick?

10:34:33 <crushedmarigolds> Yes

10:34:44 <agnes_in_wonderland_76> Sick with what?

10:34:56 <crushedmarigolds> What exactly is a baby? Before it's born?

10:35:04 <agnes_in_wonderland_76> What do you mean?

10:35:08 <crushedmarigolds> It lives off a host body, like a parasite

10:35:13 <agnes_in_wonderland_76> I suppose

10:35:28 <crushedmarigolds> A child is an infection

10:35:34 <crushedmarigolds> Like a parasite

10:35:45 <agnes_in_wonderland_76> You're saying….?

10:35:55 <crushedmarigolds> You have to become infected

10:36:04 <crushedmarigolds> Become infected with a parasite and carry the creature as if it were your child

10:36:08 <agnes_in_wonderland_76> Will it hurt?

10:36:16 <crushedmarigolds> Change always hurts

10:36:24 <crushedmarigolds> But it will give you the life you've always wanted to carry inside you

10:36:35 <agnes_in_wonderland_76> You're certain it's the only way?

10:36:42 <crushedmarigolds> It would give you exactly what you wanted.

10:36:55 <agnes_in_wonderland_76> How do you know?

10:37:12 <crushedmarigolds> I contracted a tapeworm in college during a trip to Cambodia. I know what it feels like.

10:37:23 <agnes_in_wonderland_76> What did it feel like?

10:37:35 <crushedmarigolds> Feels like you're living for something else. Makes you feel like a God, carrying something alive inside you.

10:37:44 <agnes_in_wonderland_76> Yes, that's what I wanted it to feel like

10:37:52 <crushedmarigolds> You'll think about it?

10:38:03 <agnes_in_wonderland_76> Yes

10:38:09 <agnes_in_wonderland_76> I'll think about it

10:38:16 <crushedmarigolds> I'll love you no matter what

10:38:25 <agnes_in_wonderland_76> I'll love you, too

10:38:37 <agnes_in_wonderland_76> No matter what

[<crushedmarigolds> has left the chat]
[<agnes_in_wonderland_76> has left the chat]

EMAIL FROM AGNES PETRELLA

Date: 08/02/2000
Time: 7:41 a.m.
From: Agnes Petrella <agnes_in_wonderland_76@[omitted].com>
To: Zoe Cross <crushedmarigolds@[omitted].com>
Subject: Re: Our Conversation Last Night

Zoe,

I'll do it.
Love,
Agnes

EMAIL FROM ZOE CROSS

Date: 08/02/2000
Time: 10:08 a.m.
From: Zoe Cross <crushedmarigolds@[omitted].com>
To: Agnes Petrella
<agnes_in_wonderland_76@[omitted].com>
Subject: Re: Our Conversation Last Night

Good. I'm glad to hear it.

Now, we have to be as precise as possible when executing this plan.

It's not as simple as going to your local butcher and asking for his leanest cut of beef tenderloin. There's, of course, the possibility this won't work and will negatively impact your health.

If you're serious about going forward with this, then you're going to have to neglect any semblance of hygiene or formality when preparing to eat.

Of course, there are methods by which doctors can remove parasites from their human host; however, there's no conclusive way to actually contract the organism.

So, much of what I'm about to tell you is in no way a conclusive way to contract a parasite, but rather ways by which a host may become infected with a parasite.

You'll need to go to your local town market and ask for a pound of uncooked beef. After you've acquired the meat, you need to return home and leave the beef in a place where it won't be disturbed. Leave it outside.

It won't be long before all kinds of insects will arrive, a glittering haze swallowing the portion of meat until they've finally nourished themselves and laid their eggs deep in its brawn.

After two days of waiting, you're to go outside and locate the sun-cooked meat.

Though it may disgust you, you're to take a knife and fork and hack throw the uncooked beef, slice off a small piece, and consume it.

You're to do this until the meat is completely gone and you're fully fed.

You may want to throw up after you've eaten. You may feel as though you need to. I urge you to keep as much of it down as possible – that's the only way this will work.

And, of course, you want this to work, don't you?

EMAIL FROM AGNES PETRELLA

Date: 08/05/2000
Time: 9:07 p.m.
From: Agnes Petrella <agnes_in_wonderland_76@[omitted].com>
To: Zoe Cross <crushedmarigolds@[omitted].com>
Subject: It's finished

It's over now. The worst part is behind me.

Chewing on that – the way the little eggs burst between my teeth like sunflower seeds. I'm getting ahead of myself. I'll bet you want to know how it happened.

I did exactly what you said. I went into town and visited the local market – a horrible place I worked over the summer when I was a teenager. Haven't been there in several years, but I remember the butcher there – this giant man with a pockmarked face dressed in a bloodstained apron.

He greeted me at the counter.

"How's your mother?" he asked, leaning over and exposing the dark stains beneath both of his arms.

I made some bland comment about how well she's been (after all, how am I supposed to know?), and I asked him how his daughters are – I remember they were in preschool when I worked there.

When we were finally past the painful pleasantries, I asked him for a cut of sirloin steak.

"Just the one?" he asked me.

I nodded.

When he was done packaging it, it was as neatly packaged as a Christmas present. I recall marveling at the wrapping paper. I remember how when I was little, I thought exquisitely wrapped slices of meat resembled something too graceful to eat, as if it were the organ of an angel – the innards of some divine being far too consecrated to consume.

I returned home and I unwrapped the meat from its packaging. It was as dark red as some rare tropical plant. I lifted the piece of meat from the counter, inhaling its scent. I imagined myself biting into it, my teeth chewing through the toughness as matter separated as if it were damp cotton.

I threw the sirloin on a dinner plate and crept outside

into the backyard where I set it down behind a small tree near the fence.

Then, I waited.

Every morning I would go to the kitchen window and watch as little bugs swarmed over the fresh plate of meat, a dim cloud of insects collecting as if it were carrion's shadow – tiny winged mourners to prepare and embalm the recently deceased.

Finally, at the end of the second day, I made my way out to the tree and half expected the plate to be gone completely thanks to one of nature's little trespassers. But, miraculously, it was still there.

After swatting away some of the flies glued to the meat, I ferried it back into the kitchen and started to inspect my meal.

The sun had drained it of most of its color, little thatches of blight creeping along the edges of the uncooked steak. Ribbons of exposed tissue sprouted along the meat's surface like slashes from a knife on human skin and burrowing deep inside the yawning crevices were white maggots.

I nearly retched at the sight.

But I thought of you and knew you would want me to go through with it.

So, I took a knife and fork from the cupboard and sawed through the uncooked beef. When I was finished, I speared the piece with my fork. It was then that I noticed a tiny maggot – no bigger than the tip of a dressmaker's thimble – squirming across the piece of meat.

Even a carcass can carry life, so why not me?

Before I allowed my mind to wander too freely, I took

a bite. It was like chewing on cooked rubber, little maggots squishing like jelly between my teeth as I gnawed.

I took another bite. And then, another.

I vomited once.

But I kept eating. Just like you told me to.

Finally, the plate was clear.

I swallowed, my whole body shuddering at the acrid taste.

Now, I suppose we wait. That's all we can do.

Just think, everything could be different for me tomorrow. My whole life could change. I hope it does.

EMAIL FROM ZOE CROSS

Date: 08/07/2000
Time: 8:33 a.m.
From: Zoe Cross <crushedmarigolds@[omitted].com>
To: Agnes Petrella
<agnes_in_wonderland_76@[omitted].com>
Subject: Re: It's finished

Hey,

You weren't on Instant Messenger last night. I waited for you.

Is everything OK?

I've been thinking of you.

I still can't quite believe you went through with it. I never thought you would. I thought you'd ask to not see me again or tell me off when I first suggested it.

But you want this bad enough. I can tell.

Write me back so I know you're OK.

Love,
Zoe

EMAIL FROM AGNES PETRELLA

<u>Date:</u> 08/08/2000
<u>Time:</u> 6:41 p.m.
<u>From:</u> Agnes Petrella <agnes_in_wonderland_76@[omitted].com>
<u>To:</u> Zoe Cross <crushedmarigolds@[omitted].com>
<u>Subject:</u> Re: It's finished

It didn't work.

After everything I've done, and it didn't work.

My roommate took me to the hospital the other night because I couldn't stop vomiting. They ran a bunch of tests and kept me there for observation. But I don't think it's happened.

They would've told me, right?

They would've seen some sign – something in the tests. I don't know how quickly it works or what it might show up as, but they would've told me they found something inside me after so many tests.

There's no point to anything.

It doesn't matter. It's always never mattered.

Did I ever tell you the one about the cat and the priest?

You know, it's been so cold lately. I read somewhere online that you should always check underneath your car before you start it because sometimes little animals like to nest under there to get warm.

Well, my roommate was working late one night, and

we needed bread and eggs. So, I got in the car and drove down the street to the market on the corner of Ashworth and Beaumont. Picked up the bread and eggs – and a few other things I needed.

As I'm walking through the store, I notice there's a priest, dressed in his robes, also shopping.

He's dressed in expensive-looking black and has the white collar around his neck. He looks so out of place in this labyrinth of linoleum and fluorescent lighting, like a lost member of some celestial court.

So, I start to follow him through the store. I don't know why. I just do.

I'm about to go up to him and say something – I have no idea what I'm going to say – but he dashes to the Express checkout line before I can get his attention. So, after I'm done buying my groceries, I try to catch him out at his car in the parking lot.

But, once again, he's too quick for me and he's already ducking into the driver's seat. I happen to glance beneath his car because I see something moving there in the light.

Something curled beneath one of the tires.

It's a stray cat with a bright orange tail. I wave at him to stop, but he doesn't see me. And the car's tires slide right over the cat.

The cat lays there, dead. Ropes of its intestines pushed out through its open mouth. Its ribcage – flattened like a sheet of paper.

I wave at the priest, "Stop. Please."

He does. Rolls down the window. I say, "you just ran over this poor cat."

He doesn't even bother to look at it. He merely looks at me and asks, "Does it matter?"

And with that, he cranks up his window and speeds off down the lane. And as I'm left standing there with the squeezed out remains of that dead cat, I wonder to myself, "Does it matter? Does any of this really matter?"

The answer's no.

The answer's always been no.

PART FIVE
GRACIOUS HOST

EMAIL FROM AGNES PETRELLA

Date: 08/12/2000
Time: 11:29 a.m.
From: Agnes Petrella <agnes_in_wonderland_76@[omitted].com>
To: Zoe Cross <crushedmarigolds@[omitted].com>
Subject: Things may be changing

It may be finally happening for us.

I woke up this morning and found myself unable to pull myself away from kneeling before the toilet.

I have the most intense abdominal pain I've ever felt. Worse than my usual period cramps. It feels like a cat's claw raking through my insides and readjusting what it finds there.

I think it's finally happened: I'm carrying life inside me.

It's yours, too.
Ours.

EMAIL FROM ZOE CROSS

Date: 08/12/2000
Time: 1:17 p.m.
From: Zoe Cross <crushedmarigolds@[omitted].com>
To: Agnes Petrella
<agnes_in_wonderland_76@[omitted].com>
Subject: Re: Things may be changing

Agnes,

I'm delighted to hear you're so optimistic about everything. It sounds promising, from what I can tell.

You very well could be hosting a parasite now.

The only way to actually be certain of the infection is to consult with your primary care physician.

I would make an appointment with him or her as soon as possible.

Zoe

EMAIL FROM AGNES PETRELLA

Date: 08/12/2000
Time: 2:32 p.m.
From: Agnes Petrella <agnes_in_wonderland_76@[omitted].com>
To: Zoe Cross <crushedmarigolds@[omitted].com>
Subject: Re: Things may be changing

Are you happy, my love? Please tell me you are.

EMAIL FROM ZOE CROSS

Date: 08/12/2000
Time: 3:19 p.m.
From: Zoe Cross <crushedmarigolds@[omitted].com>
To: Agnes Petrella
<agnes_in_wonderland_76@[omitted].com>
Subject: Re: Things may be changing

I'm happy if you are, my love. That's all that matters.
Let me know what the doctor says.

EMAIL FROM AGNES PETRELLA

Date: 08/15/2000
Time: 3:54 p.m.
From: Agnes Petrella <agnes_in_wonderland_76@[omitted].com>
To: Zoe Cross <crushedmarigolds@[omitted].com>
Subject: It's a boy

It's real. I can hardly believe it.

I had to sit down and compose myself when the doctor first told me.

There's a living thing inside me.

And it's ours, my love.

It's ours.

They ran some more tests – bloodwork, a stool sample,

etc. And that's when the doctor came into the room and explained I'm the host to a tapeworm.

Our child.

I know tapeworms are technically hermaphrodites and have both male and female sex organs, but wouldn't it be nice to think of it as a boy?

A son.

Our little family.

We could name him whatever we please.

What do you think of the name Finneas? I suppose we have time to think and pick out the most perfect name for our child.

I can hardly contain my excitement.

It's what I've wanted my whole life. I hope you're happy, too.

I'm sure you are.

I'll be on Instant Messenger later tonight. We can talk about names and everything else then.

Thank you for everything, my love.

Thank you for making me a mother.

INSTANT MESSAGING CONVERSATION BETWEEN AGNES AND ZOE

08/15/2000

[<crushedmarigolds> has entered the chat]
[<agnes_in_wonderland_76> has entered the chat]

10:09:12 <agnes_in_wonderland_76> You're going to be a mother!
10:09:18 <agnes_in_wonderland_76> Can you believe it?

10:09:30 <crushedmarigolds> Are you happy?

10:09:48 <agnes_in_wonderland_76> How can you even ask that? You already know I'm ecstatic. Over the moon.

10:09:56 <agnes_in_wonderland_76> Do you know what I did today?

10:10:03 <crushedmarigolds> What?

10:10:12 <agnes_in_wonderland_76> I sang

10:10:14 <agnes_in_wonderland_76> In public

10:10:19 <agnes_in_wonderland_76> People were listening, and I didn't care

10:10:26 <agnes_in_wonderland_76> I feel wonderful. The best I've felt in years. All because of you

10:10:34 <crushedmarigolds> What did the doctor say?

10:10:39 <agnes_in_wonderland_76> He prescribed me some meds

10:10:45 <agnes_in_wonderland_76> I'm not going to take them, of course

10:10:49 <agnes_in_wonderland_76> They want to kill our child

10:10:59 <agnes_in_wonderland_76> I don't even want to go out anymore

10:11:05 <crushedmarigolds> Why's that?

10:11:09 <agnes_in_wonderland_76> I want to be with you and our baby

10:11:16 <agnes_in_wonderland_76> The three of us together

10:11:22 <crushedmarigolds> But what about….

10:11:29 <agnes_in_wonderland_76> Yes?

10:11:38 <crushedmarigolds> What about when your body finally passes the tapeworm?

10:11:44 <agnes_in_wonderland_76> That's not going to happen

10:11:49 <crushedmarigolds> It's not?

10:12:02 <agnes_in_wonderland_76> I'm going to carry our child forever. He's going to always be a part of me.

10:12:09 <agnes_in_wonderland_76> That's how it's going to be, isn't it?

10:12:14 <agnes_in_wonderland_76> I'll always have a part of you inside me

10:12:19 <crushedmarigolds> But that's not the way it works

10:12:24 <agnes_in_wonderland_76> What are you trying to say?

10:12:35 <crushedmarigolds> Eventually it'll pass

10:12:46 <crushedmarigolds> You can't play the "gracious host" forever

10:12:57 <agnes_in_wonderland_76> Are you not happy?

10:13:05 <agnes_in_wonderland_76> I thought you would be

10:13:09 <crushedmarigolds> Of course, I'm happy

10:13:17 <crushedmarigolds> This is what you wanted, after all

10:13:22 <crushedmarigolds> But I don't want you to be hurt

10:13:29 <agnes_in_wonderland_76> I know you'd never hurt me

10:13:37 <crushedmarigolds> When it leaves you

10:13:44 <agnes_in_wonderland_76> It's not going to leave me

10:13:49 <agnes_in_wonderland_76> I'm going to keep it forever

10:14:09 <agnes_in_wonderland_76> Sometimes I imagine the three of us lying in bed together – your arms

wrapped around me, our beloved little worm curled like a cold, wet rope on my stomach
10:14:19 <agnes_in_wonderland_76> Wouldn't that be perfect?
10:14:27 <agnes_in_wonderland_76> Don't you dream of those things too?
10:14:35 <crushedmarigolds> I haven't been dreaming lately
10:14:45 <crushedmarigolds> I have to go get some sleep
10:14:27 <agnes_in_wonderland_76> Can't you stay?
10:14:32 <agnes_in_wonderland_76> Five more minutes?
10:14:43 <crushedmarigolds> We'll talk tomorrow. I'll send you an email
10:14:48 <agnes_in_wonderland_76> You still love me?
10:14:55 <crushedmarigolds> Yes
10:14:59 <agnes_in_wonderland_76> I love you, too
10:15:02 <agnes_in_wonderland_76> The both of us do

[<crushedmarigolds> has left the chat]
[<agnes_in_wonderland_76> has left the chat]

EMAIL FROM ZOE CROSS

Date: 08/16/2000
Time: 12:17 p.m.
From: Zoe Cross <crushedmarigolds@[omitted].com>
To: Agnes Petrella
<agnes_in_wonderland_76@[omitted].com>
Subject: I'm having second thoughts

Agnes,

This isn't an easy email for me to write. I'm afraid none of this gives me any semblance of pleasure.

If I expect total honesty and obedience from you, then you, at the very least, deserve the same amount of trustworthiness from me.

The truth is I'm worried about you. Not only your physical health, but your mental well-being as well.

If I'm being totally honest with you – some of the things I've made you do have been rooted in a place of selfishness. Some of the things I've made you do have been a result of my whims – placing bets on your endurance and wondering how far you'll go before you break.

You've proved me wrong several times, and I'm afraid much of the hardship was at your expense.

I'm not a good person. Not as good of a person as you are.

I'm ashamed to admit it, but you deserve someone who won't pretend to care for you while they are meanwhile banking on your misfortune.

Because of this, I'm thinking of ending things between us for the foreseeable future.

I know you're going to be upset. But this is for the best. I ask you to trust me.

I know I certainly don't deserve any trust given my capriciousness, but I know in time you'll come to recognize that I'm trying to help you. For the first time I'm thinking of someone other than myself. It scares me.

But letting something happen to you scares me even more.

The sad truth is I don't think I love you as much as you love me. And that's OK. That happens in relationships all the time – there's always someone who loves more than the other.

But I can't take ownership of your destruction. I want this to stop.

EMAIL FROM AGNES PETRELLA

Date: 08/16/2000
Time: 2:08 p.m.
From: Agnes Petrella <agnes_in_wonderland_76@[omitted].com>
To: Zoe Cross <crushedmarigolds@[omitted].com>
Subject: Re: I'm having second thoughts

Fuck your second thoughts.

Fuck your honesty. I don't need your honesty. I need your love, and I foolishly thought it was mine all this time.

I can't believe you're doing this to me.

I'm not some car battery you use for a couple thousand miles and then send off to the junkyard, you fucking cunt.

I know exactly what you're trying to do.

You're trying to abandon me with our child. The one you wanted as well.

This life inside me is ours. No matter what you say. No matter what you think.

It's always going to be ours.

EMAIL FROM ZOE CROSS

Date: 08/17/2000
Time: 8:43 a.m.

From: Zoe Cross <crushedmarigolds@[omitted].com>
To: Agnes Petrella
<agnes_in_wonderland_76@[omitted].com>
Subject: Re: I'm having second thoughts

I've tried to reason with you and look where it's gotten me.

Agnes, you're sick and you need help.

If you're going to continue to be so monstrous, then I have no choice but to cut all communication with you.

As far as I'm concerned, our contract is null and void.

Do not reach out to me as I will not be responding.

I sincerely hope you get the help that you need.

EMAIL FROM ZOE CROSS

Date: 08/17/2000
Time: 8:56 a.m.
From: Zoe Cross <crushedmarigolds@[omitted].com>
To: Agnes Petrella
<agnes_in_wonderland_76@[omitted].com>
Subject: Re: I'm having second thoughts

I think I did once love you.
I think I could have loved you.
But not like this.
Never like this.

EMAIL FROM AGNES PETRELLA

Date: 08/18/2000

Time: 11:09 a.m.
From: Agnes Petrella <agnes_in_wonderland_76@[omitted].com>
To: Zoe Cross <crushedmarigolds@[omitted].com>
Subject: Re: I'm having second thoughts

You'll never leave me. You love me too much.

You love our child too much.

I know you'll respond. You always will.

Because you know the life I'm carrying inside me belongs to you.

I thought of you last night.

I slept without clothes on, as we had agreed upon. The AC was running on full blast.

I didn't even care how cold it was.

I just thought of how it would feel to have you lying next to me – our child coiled inside my stomach.

EMAIL FROM AGNES PETRELLA

Date: 08/19/2000
Time: 7:43 p.m.
From: Agnes Petrella <agnes_in_wonderland_76@[omitted].com>
To: Zoe Cross <crushedmarigolds@[omitted].com>
Subject: Re: I'm having second thoughts

Please respond. It's been days since we last talked.

I want things to go back to how they were.

If you'd like me to get help, I'll get it.

Anything you say.

Just please talk to me. I can't bear being apart from you.

EMAIL FROM AGNES PETRELLA

<u>Date:</u> 08/20/2000
<u>Time:</u> 9:33 p.m.
<u>From:</u> Agnes Petrella <agnes_in_wonderland_76@[omitted].com>
<u>To:</u> Zoe Cross <crushedmarigolds@[omitted].com>
<u>Subject:</u> Something's wrong

Things have gotten worse since we last spoke.

I think there's something wrong.

It hurts me to even think it, but something's not right with our child.

I feel this intense pain all the time, as if someone were sliding a razor blade along my guts.

I don't know if I can bear it anymore. I feel like taking a pair of shears and slicing myself open.

Would you come then?

Would that get your attention?

EMAIL FROM AGNES PETRELLA

<u>Date:</u> 08/21/2000
<u>Time:</u> 6:45 p.m.
<u>From:</u> Agnes Petrella <agnes_in_wonderland_76@[omitted].com>
<u>To:</u> Zoe Cross <crushedmarigolds@[omitted].com>
<u>Subject:</u> Re: Something's wrong

Please help me.

I think something's happening to our child.

It feels like a gloved hand pushing its way through my innards and reaching down between where my legs meet.

Something's going to happen.

EMAIL FROM AGNES PETRELLA

Date: 08/21/2000
Time: 8:02 p.m.
From: Agnes Petrella <agnes_in_wonderland_76@[omitted].com>
To: Zoe Cross <crushedmarigolds@[omitted].com>
Subject: Re: Something's wrong

I passed it. Just like you said.

It's a damp, crumpled heap on the bathroom floor.

Looks like one of the ribbons my mother used to sew into my hair when I was a little girl – shiny and bright.

EMAIL FROM AGNES PETRELLA

Date: 08/21/2000
Time: 8:38 p.m.
From: Agnes Petrella <agnes_in_wonderland_76@[omitted].com>
To: Zoe Cross <crushedmarigolds@[omitted].com>
Subject: Re: Something's wrong

I wish you were here.

He's beautiful.

He has your eyes. And your smile.

I hold him in my arms and pretend he makes little cooing noises at me the way all babies do.

EMAIL FROM AGNES PETRELLA

Date: 08/21/2000
Time: 9:06 p.m.
From: Agnes Petrella <agnes_in_wonderland_76@[omitted].com>
To: Zoe Cross <crushedmarigolds@[omitted].com>
Subject: Re: Something's wrong

I take the apple peeler from the kitchen and I crawl into the bathroom closet, gently cradling our child.

I pretend I can hear the sound of him faintly breathing.

The peeler trembles in my hand.

I close my eyes, and for a moment I wonder if I truly deserve them today.

ACKNOWLEDGMENTS

If there's one thing I pride myself in, it's my inclination to be honest with readers.

I must confess, I was in such a peculiar headspace while writing this particular novella. *Things Have Gotten Worse Since We Last Spoke* is a bizarre fantasy of manipulation and depravity. You might be interested to know the very first draft of the piece was written over the course of merely five days – a nightmarish fever dream of inspiration, an arduous ordeal of painstaking creativity. Though I am and will continue to be an advocate for any artist's mental health, I quite literally pushed myself to dangerous areas of my mind during those five days of creative Armageddon.

There are many people to whom I'm forever indebted for their kindness and encouragement during and after the creation of this nasty little nugget of terror.

Of course, I'm compelled to immediately shower my beloved partner, Ali, with warmth and affection for putting up with me and suffering through my excruciating mood swings while I created this book. Also, much gratitude belongs to my mother and father for their encouragement and support. Though they may not have always understood my attraction to the ghoulish, they have gone above and beyond to see that my happiness is forever well managed.

I would be remiss if I didn't take this opportunity to thank the several beta readers I corresponded with before sending off this piece to Weirdpunk for consideration. My eternal gratefulness belongs to Kyler Fey and Erica Robyn for their intelligent and thoughtful feedback.

My heartfelt appreciation belongs to Sam Richard for believing in this macabre tale of online lust and perversion. When I first pitched the concept to him on Twitter, he immediately understood the beating, bloody heart of the story. Working with Sam has been such a seamless partnership and I am so honored to join the Weirdpunk family.

Huge thanks to my manager, Ryan Lewis, for making contacts on my behalf and helping me secure certain blurbs I would have otherwise been unable to procure.

That said, I need to take this time to thank the very kind and talented writers who read early versions of the manuscript and provided blurbs. My endless gratitude belongs to Josh Malerman, John Skipp, Max Booth III, Hailey Piper, Tyler Jones, and Ross Jeffery for their encouragement, their mentorship, and their time.

I'd like to dedicate this book to anybody who has gone searching for something, someone in the glittering darkness of cyberspace just to feel a little less lonely. Perhaps you found something truly wondrous. Perhaps you didn't. Regardless, this book belongs to you.

ABOUT THE AUTHOR

Eric LaRocca's fiction has appeared in various literary journals and anthologies in the US and abroad. He is the author of several novellas and collections including *Fanged Dandelion* and *Starving Ghosts in Every Thread*. He is represented by Ryan Lewis/Spin a Black Yarn. For more information, please follow him on Twitter @ejlarocca or visit him at ericlarocca.com.

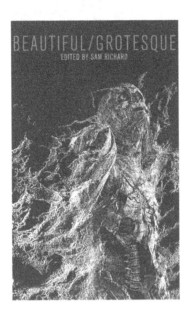

Beautiful/Grotesque - Edited by Sam Richard

Five authors of strange fiction, Roland Blackburn (*Seventeen Names For Skin*), Jo Quenell (*The Mud Ballad*), Katy Michelle Quinn (*Girl in the Walls*), Joanna Koch (*The Wingspan of Severed Hands*), and Sam Richard (*Sabbath of the Fox-Devils*) each bring you their own unique vision of the macabre and the glorious violently colliding. From full-on hardcore horror, to decadently surreal nightmares, and noir-fueled psychosis, to an eerie meditation on grief, and familial quiet horror, *Beautiful/Grotesque* guides us through the murky waters where the monstrous and the breathtaking meet.

They are all beautiful. They are all grotesque.

The Wingspan of Severed Hands by Joanna Koch

Three Women, One Battle. A world gone mad. Cities abandoned. Dreams invade waking minds. An invisible threat lures those who oppose its otherworldly violence to become acolytes of a nameless cult. As a teenage girl struggles for autonomy, a female weapons director in a secret research facility develops a living neuro-cognitive device that explodes into self-awareness. Discovering their hidden emotional bonds, all three unveil a common enemy through dissonant realities that intertwine in a cosmic battle across hallucinatory dreamscapes. Time is the winning predator, and every moment spirals deeper into the heart of the beast.

Seventeen Names for Skin by Roland Blackburn

After a cancer diagnosis gives her six-months to live, Snow Turner does what any introverted body-piercer might: hire a dark-web assassin and take out a massive life insurance policy to help her ailing father. But when a vicious attack leaves her all too alive and with a polymorphic curse, the bodies begin stacking up. As the insatiable hunger and violent changes threaten to consumer her, she learns that someone may still be trying to end her life. Can Snow keep her humanity intact, or will she tear everything she loves apart?

CPSIA information can be obtained
at www.ICGtesting.com
Printed in the USA
LVHW051757160921
697991LV00001BA/256

9 781951 658120